Where Do We Go From Here II

Jae Henderson & Mario D. King

Where Do We Go From Here II

Printed in the United States

Put It In Writing
726 North Parkway
Memphis, TN 38105

This book is dedicated to any couple who ever wondered, *Where do we go from here*? Keep the faith.

Foreword

1 Corinthians: 13 4- 7 says, "Love is patient, love is kind. It does not envy, it does not boast, it is not proud. It does not dishonor others, it is not self-seeking, it is not easily angered, it keeps no record of wrongs. Love does not delight in evil but rejoices with the truth. It always protects, always trusts, always hopes, always perseveres."

We are grateful that you decided to continue on this journey with us as we seek to illustrate what it looks like when all of those principals are at play. Relationships can become messy and complication but they can also be beautiful and breathtaking. Life is a series of decisions and it is those decisions that can determine the quality of life we will live. We implore each of you to choose wisely, especially when the lives of others are directly impacted by those decisions.

We still believe in black love. We still believe in family. We know that if we want our communities to get better we need our families to stay intact. Love is the glue that holds it together.

Because after all, life is simple. It's our bad decisions that often makes it complicated. Make a decision to treat one another with respect, have children with someone you actually want to be with and love like our community depends on it.

Jae & Mario

Chapter 1

Natalie

After an entire month in the hospital, I am being discharged. It took a while, but the doctors finally got this little guy's repeated efforts to enter the world under control. When I was admitted, I was only 6 months, and that is much too early to give birth. I was told that it might be caused by stress, and I had to agree to complete bed rest to get discharged. I readily agreed. I was sick of this place. I'm sick of being poked and prodded all times of the day and night. I'm sick of bland food, but most of all, I missed my first baby, Pepper. Dogs aren't allowed in the hospital, but Marcus snuck him in a couple of times to bring me some joy. Marcus has been amazing throughout my entire hospital stay. He, his family, and my godmother make sure that I know I'm not alone. It's been a beautiful experience as far as hospital stays go.

I'm just glad the contractions are under control now. I don't really have any stress, but what I do have is guilt. I feel horrible about what my little brother, Jessie, and my best friend, Manny, did to Marcus. He still has headaches, and sometimes he even has nightmares that he's being attacked while jogging. I also feel slightly guilty about the role I played in getting rid of Marcus's ex-girlfriend, Chanel. The night they broke up, I knew she was coming over. It was obvious. He had wine, soft music playing, and rose petals all over the place. He never did those things for me.

I wanted her to come in and see us together inappropriately. I used Marcus's care for me and his high libido as weapons to make it happen. I was wrong, but I needed her out of the life of my future husband. My plan worked. She's gone, and Marcus has been giving me and our child his full attention. The only problem is my conscience is eating me alive. Why couldn't I let go of the guilt? Especially since it was both of those actions that landed Marcus right by my side, and I think he's almost to the point of giving us a try. He keeps using the words "us," "we," and "our." He hasn't officially made me his girlfriend, but I know it's coming. I tried to get Jessie to let me tell Marcus what happened to give me some relief, but he pointed out how much he had at stake. If Marcus decided to press charges, Jessie could lose the endorsement deal he just got with Muscle Man Protein Powder, and he's currently being considered for a role in a new independent film.

Jessie also told me that I could lose Marcus. I don't ever want that to happen. I'm in love with that man and we, me and this baby, need him. Marcus is even moving me in with him so he can take care of us while I'm on bed rest. He didn't want me home alone, and he didn't want to have to keep traveling back and forth from his place to mine.

As I signed the last bit of discharge paperwork, Marcus entered my hospital room to get me and take me to *our* house. I loved the way that sounded. He had been at my apartment getting some of my things to make *our* house seem more like home.

He came in and gave me a quick peck on the lips. "You ready to go, baby?"

Baby. I loved when he used terms of endearment. "Yup. I can't wait to get out of here," I said.

"Me and you both. I'll be much more comfortable at my place, and I'm sure you will too. Sleeping on this hospital couch was killing my back. But before we go, I need to ask you something."

I looked into those brown eyes of his adoringly and said. "Sure, Handsome. Ask me anything."

He reached into his jacket pocket and pulled something out. "What was this doing at your place?"

I looked down and in his hand was his wallet. The black leather wallet Jessie and Manny stole the day they beat him up in the park and made it look like a robbery.

It still contained his debit and credit cards, driver's license and a picture of his little sister, Mia. I looked at the wallet, and I looked at him. I suddenly went mute. I wanted to say something, but the words wouldn't form. My chest felt tight, and the room was spinning.

"I found it while I was going through some of your drawers looking for pajamas for you and Pepper. Is there something you want to tell me, Natalie?"

I opened my mouth to tell him I had nothing to do with it. I wanted to tell him that Jessie and Manny acted on their own accord. It was in retaliation for the pain he caused me when I found out about Chanel. He wasn't supposed to have a girlfriend while I was carrying his child. Instead, what came out was a piercing scream in reaction to the excruciating pain shooting through my abdomen.

"Oh shit! I'm sorry, Natalie. Calm down. I didn't mean to upset you," he said.

I shot him a dirty look, reached over, and pushed the button for the nurse. Someone responded quickly and said, "Yes, Ms. Natalie. How can I help you?" I had been there so long the entire staff knew my name.

"Call the doctor. I think I'm going into labor again!" I screamed as another pain ripped through me.

Marcus stood there with a look of horror and shame on his face. He was there when the doctor said that I needed to try my best not to get upset. Was he trying to hurt our baby on purpose? Did he want answers so badly that he would jeopardize the life of our unborn child?

As the doctors and nurses rushed in, I screamed, "Get out! What the hell is wrong with you? I hate you! Get out!"

The doctor looked at both of us and said, "I don't know what's going on here, Mr. Colbert, but you are upsetting my patient, and you need to leave."

Marcus didn't budge. One of the nurses who had become my friend, Nurse Brandy, walked toward him, got in his face, and started backing him toward the door.

"I didn't mean to. It was an accident," he said. "I'm sorry. I can't leave. I need to know what's going on with my son."

The doctors put me back in the bed and reinserted an IV into my arm. A tear rolled out of my left eye as I realized that I wasn't being discharged from the hospital. I hated this place, but at that moment, there was one thing—or should I say *person*—I hated more.

"I'll give you an update as soon as I can, but for now, you have to follow the doctor's orders and leave, Marcus."

Marcus took one more step back which placed him outside the doorway and into the hall. Nurse Brandy then shut the door in his face.

I screamed as another painful contraction took hold of me.

"Natalie," said the doctor, "I don't think we're going to be able to stop it this time. You're about to go into labor. Do you want Marcus here?"

It was because of his stupid ass I was going into premature labor. "No! Keep him away from me. Call my godmother, Dr. Adina Frank. Her practice is nearby. That's the only person I want in the room with me."

I prayed silently. *God, I'm sorry for all I've done, but please don't take it out on my child. Let me have a healthy baby, please.*

Chapter 2

Marcus

With my eyes closed, I sat—relaxed. My head was nestled comfortably between the edge of my seat and the window to my right. My mood mirrored the song that was playing within my headset—melancholy. I was startled as the woman sitting next to me nudged my shoulder. Reluctantly, I opened my eyes and turned to my left. My eyes met with the redheaded woman reading a book about love languages. I pulled back one of the speakers of my headphones from my ear as I replied, "How can I help you?"

She put a bookmarker that was decorated with flower petals inside her book as she closed it. Then, she placed one of her hands to her chest. I immediately noticed the perfectly fitted diamond ring resting snug on her ring finger as she said, "I don't mean to intrude." She paused as if she was carefully choosing her words to follow. "Would it be too much of a burden, my dear, if I asked you to lower the level of your music a tad bit?"

Looking into her blue eyes that were accompanied by crow's feet, I replied, "Not a problem at all, ma'am." She continued to stare at me as if I was supposed to continue with the conversation. One of the first thoughts that ran through my mind was, *Why would a woman who had to be on the north side of sixty-five need to read a book about love languages?* If I was in a better mood, I would have entertained an amusing conversation with her, but I wasn't.

I lowered the volume and proceeded to look out the window. My body jerked due to some slight turbulence. I always thought it was funny seeing the world from a bird's-eye view. You can see the actual design of the landscapes. You can see how the pieces of the puzzle were put together. I always wondered if that was the same perspective God or the angels have, when they see us from a bird's-eye view. At that particular point in time, my life was much like that airplane ride—smooth—then full of turbulence.

I was headed to Seattle for a conference for work. Out of all the places in the world, it just had to be Seattle. When I told Natalie about the trip, of course she felt a little uneasy—apprehensive about it. After all, she knew that this was the new residence of my ex-girlfriend—Lisa.

Natalie and I haven't been on the best of terms as of late. During her extended stay in the hospital, I went to her place and ran across my wallet while packing her some pajamas. This wallet was supposed to have been stolen during the robbery and assault I received while jogging in the park last year. When I questioned her about it, she began to have some severe contractions. The doctors rushed in and rushed me out. We thought she was about to go into labor. Thankfully, the quick response by the excellent staff in the hospital enabled them to get things under control once again. I was pleased to know that my little man was still safe. I decided to ease off the questioning about my wallet for another day. My main concern and focus was about the well-being of Natalie while she was carrying our child. However, I'm having real trust issues with her right now.

I arrived at the Sheraton Seattle Hotel close to noon. It had just begun to rain. I stepped out of my taxi. My jogging suit was slightly damp from the leak in the backseat window. As the taxi driver pulled my luggage from the trunk, I exhaled deeply, immediately followed by an even deeper inhale. I enjoyed taking in the air of a new city. It was almost as if it was a fresh new start. The short, stubby man with a too-small fedora resting atop his head handed me my luggage. I gave him a tip and proceeded to walk inside the lobby of the hotel.

Standing at the front desk, I had some small talk with the nice-looking brunette as she tried to find me an open room since check-in was not until 3 p.m. I picked up a flyer that advertised some of the nearby attractions: The Seattle Art Museum and Pike Place Market were highlighted as "must-visit" places. *Interesting*, I said to myself as I read over some of the history of the market.

"Mr. Colbert, I have some great news. We do have a room open. You will be on the twentieth floor. How many keys would you need?" I felt relieved that I didn't have to wait any longer. "One—I just need one."

As soon as I stepped one foot into my room, my phone buzzed. It was Natalie. I had been ignoring her calls and texts today. I knew it was childish on my behalf, but men actually do have feelings too. I admit, I was still in my feelings about her making that outlandish scene at the hospital. All I did was question why my wallet was at her place of residence. It just didn't make sense to me, and it still doesn't. I've been trying to fit the pieces of the puzzle together, but the parts have been misaligning.

I was anticipating a little jet lag within the next couple of hours so I decided to go ahead and find me a bite to eat. Since it was now raining cats and dogs, I didn't plan on leaving the hotel, so I ordered room service. Now that my belly was about to be satisfied, I needed to go over some paperwork for the following day's meeting. However, I couldn't stop thinking about my future little boy. I began to envision what he would look like: his round little head, kinky hair, snub nose, and puffy little eyes I was sure would make a person's heart bleed. I hadn't felt that feeling before. I was thinking about something—someone—that *I* helped to create. I hoped that this new bundle of joy would grow and thrive within a loving home—a home that he would be proud of. At that moment, I realized that I was being what I accused Natalie of being—petty. No longer could *we* be selfish in our ways. We now had someone else acting as an equalizer—a middleman of sorts. Therefore, I decided to return her call.

"How was the flight?" she said in what sounded to me like a somber mood.

I exhaled. "It was fine." Short and to the point is how I wanted to reply. I wanted to keep the lines of communication open, but I also wanted her to know that I hadn't forgotten about what she did, and the mystery of my wallet was still in the air.

"Trenton has been kicking all day today. I guess he's missing his daddy."

I flashed a smile. Mood brightened a little. "That's good to hear."

Empty silence was between us.

"So . . . What's on the agenda tomorrow?" Natalie asked, breaking the silence.

"More than likely, I'll be cooped up in a room full of people with their noses in the air and asses out."

She laughed.

"Well, are y'all going out for dinner afterward?"

I understood that question as her trying to probe to see how much free time I would have on my hands while on this 3-day stay in Seattle.

"I'm not sure, but more than likely we should."

We talked a bit more—both of us being careful with our choice of words and topics. Now stretched comfortably across the king-sized bed in my room, our conversation was interrupted by a knock at the door. I proceed to tell Natalie that I would call her back as my food had arrived. The words "I love you" didn't escape either one of our lips. It was simply—talk to you later—and a short—good-bye.

The New York Strip Steak and Spinach Mash had me full as a tick. After a long hot shower, I decided to indulge in a little more *me* time before I prepped for tomorrow's conference. I was presenting alongside Kristine, a tempting blond with classic and captivating perfume. I opened my laptop and browsed through my normal sites: ESPN, BBC, The Atlantic, Amazon, YouTube, Facebook, Twitter, LinkedIn, and DatPiff. After nearly an hour of uninterrupted site surfing, I reluctantly reached for my briefcase. *This work isn't gonna work itself,* I thought. I patted my belly as it was still stuffed to its normal capacity.

While listening to the raindrops tap aggressively at my window intermingled with beautiful flashes of lightning, I heard a *ping* sound on my phone. Uncomfortably, I reach over the pillows stretching to the nightstand and unattached my phone from the charger: 57 percent battery life. I turned it on to see a new notification from Instagram letting me know that one of my Facebook friends was now on there. The name appeared as: *LBurns85*. I didn't even have to see the pic to know who it was. It was Lisa. Coincidence? Fate? Temptation? Test? I began to question it all. We followed each other in less than 2 minutes. Staring at the screen for what seemed like 3 hours, I had a multitude of butterflies fluttering around in my stomach. Heart rate increase, widened eyes with a rather taut expression—was the energy that was bouncing off me within that small room. It felt as if a large lump was in my throat. I attempted to swallow. Then that's when I got it—a direct message (DM) that stated:

I SAW YOUR POST ON FB. RU IN SEATTLE NOW? HOW LONG? WE SHOULD TALK? MAYBE? YOU LOOK NICE ON YOUR PROFILE PIC.

Chapter 3

Natalie

Just when Marcus and I were getting along so well, he had to find that wallet. I understand him wanting answers, but what made him think asking me when I was about to be discharged from the hospital after almost going into labor multiple times was the appropriate time to ask? The doctor told him I wasn't supposed to be upset, and because of him, I went into labor . . . AGAIN. I thought this little guy was going to have to vacate early this time, but my doctors were able to keep the bun warming in the oven.

I don't blame him for being mad. Hell, *I* was mad. I truly was about to have this baby without him in the room. He would have missed out on the birth of his first child, and that offense might have been unforgiveable. Thank God I didn't deliver!

I've been at his place for about a month now. I practically had to beg my doctor to discharge me. I promised him that at the first sign of trouble I'd come back. But I had to get out of there, even if it was only for a couple of days. Being in the hospital that long will make you go stir-crazy. Thankfully, I hadn't had any signs of trouble. The baby is due sometime in early March, after Valentine's Day but before Mother's Day. Valentine's Day: the day for couples and lovers. I really don't know what to call me and Marcus. I guess we're a couple, but we never really made it official. One day it just became understood that he and I were together, and we were going to try to make it work for the sake of our child. I was patient. I was kind. I was loving. He seems to have finally got his last girlfriend, Chanel, out of his system. He was finally able to see the woman who had been standing in front of him all along—me. We haven't had sex in months because of the pregnancy, but before this last false labor, we were being very affectionate. We kissed, cuddled, and fondled on a regular basis. He rubbed my feet, my stomach, and anything else I said needed some attention. He read and talked to the baby often. He even told me he loved me a few times. I know he's not *in love* with me . . . yet. But I have no doubt he loves me. He also loves that he is about to be a father.

Since I've been at his place, Marcus has been cordial but the affection is almost zero. He doesn't even sleep with me. He gave me his bed so I could have plenty of room, and he sleeps in the spare bedroom. He'll stay in the room with me if I ask him, but I try not to. I want him to stay because he wants to lie next to me not because I requested it. The bed is king-sized. There's plenty of room for both of us. Pepper sleeps at my feet like he does at home, but it's not the same. Damn! I get it! I messed up! Keeping him out of the delivery room was a no-no. Not to mention he still needs to know why his wallet was at my house hidden in a drawer behind my vibrator. What was he doing in that drawer anyway? He was just supposed to be getting me some pajamas. I told him they were in the dresser not the chest of drawers. I think Marcus is waiting for me to bring it up, but if the conversation doesn't go well, I could end up in labor again. I can't risk that. I'd rather just table it until my baby boy is here. Besides, I don't know how to answer his questions without incriminating my brother and

Manny. Marcus isn't going to understand that they wanted to teach him a lesson for breaking my heart. I didn't tell them to. They acted on their own, and they beat him up pretty badly. I feel guilty, but what if Marcus decides to press charges? My brother's career as a professional bodybuilder has taken off like a rocket. He just signed his second endorsement deal and won his fifth first-place trophy. And my boy Manny, he and his girlfriend are expecting a baby. That boy is going to have three kids by three different women, and he isn't even 35 yet. Manny's a good guy, but I need him to pick a woman and stay with her. This is not a good time for either of them to go to jail.

I felt Trenton kick. Ouch! I swear sometimes I think that boy has on army boots in there. I smiled and then laughed. The mere thought of this sweet child who is zapping all the energy out of me and causing me to be on complete bed rest brings me massive amounts of joy. Marcus picked the name. He asked me what my mother's name was and when I told him Trena, he said that we should name him Trenton in honor of her. So Trenton Montgomery—in honor of his father—Colbert it is. I wish my mother was still alive so she could meet him. Actually—him and Marcus. I think she'd approve of both. I hate that Marcus's job called him away. He hasn't even been gone a full 24 hours, and I'm missing him already. I snuggled my face into one of the beige decorative pillows on his king-sized bed. It smelled just like him. Pleasing, sexy, strong.

Not only did Marcus have to leave while I'm having a high-risk pregnancy, but he had to go to Seattle, the home of his other ex-girlfriend. It's crazy. Marcus gave both her and Chanel the official *title* of girlfriend freely, but I'm the woman who's having his baby, and I had to fight for it. I'm trying hard not to let it bother me, but he was in love with her. Head over heels in love and he was going to ask her to marry him if she hadn't moved. I took a moment to say a small prayer asking God to make sure Marcus behaves himself. I know he has needs, and I haven't been able to attend to them fully. I do what I can, and he hasn't complained, but I know he's used to getting some loving on the regular. The thought of someone else touching his delectable body sickens me. It's not easy being in love with a man who isn't in love with you. If I'm lucky, this baby will bring us closer together. That's why I have to do everything the doctor says, because I have to deliver a healthy baby boy at all costs.

Marcus's mother is staying at his condo with me while he's gone. I love that woman like family. She and Marcus's father have been so good to me. She's in the kitchen right now fixing me a late dinner. I wasn't hungry today, but she kept insisting I eat until I agreed to let her fix me something. I wouldn't mind calling her my mother-in-law one day. Not one bit.

She walked into the room with a tray of food. "Sweetheart, it's time to eat. You and my grandbaby need your strength."

"Yes, ma'am." The aroma from the smothered chicken, mashed potatoes with gravy, and greens she brought in smelled divine. She must have brought it with her when she came over. My mouth started salivating. So much for not being hungry.

Mrs. Colbert waited for me to get comfortable, then set the tray beside me and went to the kitchen to get me a beverage. My stomach is so big that I couldn't possibly put it on my lap. I put a piece of smothered chicken in my mouth and almost started shouting. It was seasoned just right and absolutely delicious! Then I heard the doorbell ring. I wasn't expecting any company, but maybe it was Mr. Montgomery or Marcus's little sister coming by. Since I couldn't drive I'd been letting her keep my car. She is a senior in high school and very active. With Mrs. Colbert at the condo looking after me often, having my car allowed her to still get to all her extracurricular activities without depending on her mom to take her. Mr. Colbert was at work most of the day.

After Mrs. Colbert opened the door, I distinctly heard a woman's voice. Mrs. Colbert said something, and then the door slammed. Whoever it was, *she* was not welcome. Mrs. Colbert looked upset when she came back to the room.

"Who was that?" I asked with a mouthful of mashed potatoes.

"No one, dear. Just some child trying to sell some chocolate. I told them it's too late to be knocking on people's doors. How's the food?"

"It's divine. Thank you for coming over to take care of me. You have no idea how much it means to me, Marcus, and the baby."

"Nonsense, child. That's what grandmothers are for. Besides, I like you, Natalie, and I think you're good for my son. Don't you worry that pretty little head of yours. Everything is going to be all right once little Trenton gets here. You just wait and see."

I hoped she was right. I desperately needed and wanted the Marcus who wanted to be close to me and touch me back. I knew she was lying about the chocolate because if there had been a child selling chocolate she would have bought several bars, and we would have eaten them together while watching a movie. I decided not to press her about it. Besides, I was busy eating.

"Thank you," I said. "What happened to my drink?"

"Oh, I'm sorry, sweetheart. I'll be right back."

I suddenly had a weird feeling that something was wrong with my man. Call it women's intuition or some sixth sense. I had just talked to him shortly after he landed a couple of hours ago. Everything seemed fine. I picked up my phone and looked at one of my apps. Interesting. Then I texted him.

THINKING OF YOU. I HOPE YOU'RE OKAY. GOOD LUCK TOMORROW, HANDSOME. WE LOVE YOU. GOOD NIGHT.

Just as Mrs. Colbert returned with a Sprite, he texted back.

THANKS. EVERYTHING IS FINE. DON'T LET MY MOTHER STUFF YOU. I KNOW HOW SHE LOVES TO FEED YOU. I LOVE YOU 2. GOOD NIGHT.

I smiled as I put another bite of food in my mouth. Those three words always made my world seem right. Suddenly, the food tasted even more delicious than it did before.

Chapter 4

Marcus

Temptation has always been the precursor to deceit, lies, pleasure, and ultimately, regret. Night had fallen, and my flesh desired the love that once lived within my heart—Lisa. Similar to the heart, we all understand that the flesh wants what the flesh wants. However—the flesh can be deceiving. It can create an illusion or fantasy of sorts within the mind. That delusion deters the heart from the truth. As an adult, you must know how to decipher between the flesh and the heart. This is the area that I still struggle with.

Not too long after I received the DM from Lisa, Natalie sent me her good night sentiments. The emotional roller coaster that I've been going through with Natalie has been getting the best of me as of late. In some cases, I'm a shell of my former self: both good and bad. In some ways, communicating with Lisa provided me with some sense of normalcy. I needed that. I needed to have that feeling again. I needed that feeling of trust, openness, and urgency—the urgency to feel wanted and desired without all the additional prepackaged BS that usually comes with it. In essence, I needed something that felt *real*.

My eyes continued to be fixated on the ceiling. Mind drifting, nerves fluttering. I couldn't quite understand how I seemed to always find myself in situations that are usually reserved for the clinically insane. Over time, I've learned to deal with my faults, mistakes, and imperfections. However, the way in which I dealt with them always ended with me hurting the ones who seemed to love me the most.

With my arms extended and my head resting atop my hands, I closed my eyes in search of some type of peace of mind. It couldn't have been any more than 5 minutes before I felt my phone vibrating within the sheets. I surveyed the large bed in search for it. Searching for a vibrating phone always felt like a wild witch hunt. I don't know which is worst: searching for a vibrating phone or a remote control. Nevertheless, I found it at the edge of the bed near the foot.

A new message alert flashed across the screen: SLEEP?

I fully understood that if I acknowledged the message, that would lead me to entering the point of no return. Once the faucet of lust and desire is turned on, it's difficult to turn it off.

I sent the following message back:

CAN'T SLEEP. WHY ARE YOU STILL UP?

Now sitting up, resting my back against the padded headboard, my eyes caught the clock to my left. It was a little past midnight, and I was in no rush to go to sleep. I reached for the remote to catch up on some sports highlights. I received another message.

WANNA TALK?

My number had changed since Lisa and I last spoke telephonically. After getting serious with Natalie, I decided to change my number. I was beginning to shift my focus on a future with Natalie. I couldn't do that with having instant access to Lisa and Chanel and vice versa.

Foolishly, I responded:

SURE, I WOULDN'T MIND THAT. CALL ME AT (615) 245-1311.

Her reply caught me totally off guard.

I DON'T NEED YOUR NUMBER. WHAT HOTEL ARE YOU STAYING AT?

At that moment, I knew that it was going to be a long night.

I had just stepped out of the shower when I heard a subtle knock at the door. My towel was wrapped snuggly around my waist. Droplets of water trailed behind me as I walked toward the door. My heart raced. Anxiety was getting the best of me. I peeped through the peephole before I proceeded to open the door. Hiding my body behind the door I warned, "Hey, I just got out of the shower. Give me 3 seconds to grab some pants and shirt."

She forced her way in as she jokingly replied, "You're kidding, right? I've seen you 100 times over." She then playfully placed her hands over her eyes and continued, "I'll be a good girl. I'm not looking. You go ahead and get as fully dressed as you feel you need to."

I used to love her playful spirit. It always made my heart melt like butter.

"No peeking," I replied returning the playfulness.

As I got dressed I could feel her eyes on me. Stress had been taking a toll on me not only mentally, but physically. I had dropped about 10 pounds in the course of a month. However, the slight weight loss made me seem more toned than usual, so I wasn't complaining too much.

Looking in the mirror, my eyes caught Lisa peeking through her hands. I smiled. I was now calm. The nervousness and anxiety I was previously feeling had disappeared. As I patted the last remnants of water from my back, I watched as Lisa made herself comfortable on my bed. She flopped up and down testing the firmness of the mattress. Her long black hair was in a side ponytail draped over her left shoulder. She was wearing some pink pants with a blue shoulder sweater. Her collarbone was exposed. She used to love when I nibbled on her shoulder blade. I could smell her perfume from across the room. It wasn't too overbearing. She smelled sweet—edible.

She lay back and extended her body across the bed and said, "You remember how much fun we used to have in hotels back home?"

I smiled as I immediately had some sentimental, yet funny, flashbacks. I nodded as I replied, "Yeah—I remember."

I walked toward the bed contemplating where I needed to sit. I didn't want the moment to feel awkward. I also didn't want to send the wrong signal. Then I thought to myself, *She pressed for this meeting.* I decided to take a seat at the foot of the bed right next to Lisa. Her legs dangled freely at the foot. Her pants hugged her curvaceous hips and thick thighs. I was fighting every tempted bone in my body not to take my hand and gracefully rub her thighs. She proceeded to sit up to match my posture.

Her hands relaxed in her lap. She exhaled. The scent from her breath was that of spearmint. "So what's been eating you?" she asked.

I rubbed my hands over my untidy head as I replied, "I don't know where to start."

She stood to her feet and walked toward the mini wet bar and grabbed the half bottle of red wine that sat atop the refrigerator. Holding the bottle in the air, Lisa said, "This should be the perfect way to start."

"I couldn't agree more," I replied.

She grabbed two glasses. I listened as the red wine seductively moved its way to the bottom of my glass. Before Lisa arrived, I had cut the television off. The only sound was that of the storm that was continuing to sing outside my hotel window. With a glass of wine in hand, Lisa was standing in front of the window looking out into a world that used to belong to both of us. She removed her sneakers from her feet—toes exposed. I immediately began to think about how her feet used to swell when it rained. I would have to rub the pain away. I then wondered, *Who's rubbing the pain away now?*

She walked back toward me.

"Somebody is getting a little gray hair," she said as she ran her hands over my untidy head.

"Ha. You got jokes, I see."

"No jokes. Just observant."

There was a flash of awkward silence between us.

Lisa exhaled again and asked, "So—how are things with you and what's-her-face?"

"Natalie?"

"Yeah—*Natalie*."

I hunched my shoulders. "I mean, it's going. It's a little complicated right now, but we're maintaining."

She chuckled. "Marcus Colbert and *Complications?* No. I never would have guessed it," she said in a sarcastic tone.

I playfully nudged her on the shoulder. "You're just a regular comedian tonight, huh?"

We continued with some more small talk before she hit me with it.

"I can't believe you're about to be a daddy." She playfully nudged me on the shoulder and continued, "You must be so excited. That's all you used to talk about back when—"

Cutting her off I replied, "We don't have to go down memory lane."

She nodded. "I understand. Fair enough." She took a sip of wine. "So, do you know if it's a boy or a girl?"

"It's a boy."

"Wow. That's *so* awesome, Marcus," she said with more sarcasm.

"What about you?" I asked.

"In terms of what?" she replied.

"Are you dating anyone?"

She stood to her feet again and began to stretch. Her sweater raised just high enough for me to get a glimpse of her flat stomach and flower tattoo. "Honestly, I don't have the time."

Those words sounded too familiar. Her not having time was what ultimately ended our relationship. Her *time* in her career was more important than the time she could have had with me.

She turned around and faced me. Our eyes connected. No words were spoken. She bit the bottom of her lip and looked away as if she was deep in thought. She returned and fixed her eyes with mine again. She walked closer to me slowly. I extended my arms to pull her in closer. My hands were now resting on the small of her back. Her body language was welcoming my embrace. Her left hand began to slowly caress my face as if she was washing my stress away. When her fingers graced my lips, I pulled her closer—causing her to stumble and fall atop me. There we were: face-to-face and heart-to-heart.

A laundry list of memories rested within us. Memories that neither one of us was ready and willing to let go of—permanently. Therefore, we let the mood of the moon and the sound of the rain dictate where we were going the rest of the night.

Chapter 5

Natalie

It was the wee hours of the morning. My little prince was restless and wouldn't let me sleep. I just couldn't get comfortable. I tried lying on my left side, my right side, and my back, but he wouldn't stop squirming and kicking. The kicking was constant, like he was marching in the army. Left, right, left . . . or at least that's what it felt like. He'd stop for a few minutes and then start back up again.

"What is going on with you?" I asked my abdomen.

I assumed Trenton couldn't sleep for the same reason I couldn't—his daddy wasn't near. Even though some nights we slept in separate rooms, just knowing he was near was comforting. Also, every night before I went to sleep he came to say good night to me and the baby. No matter how mad he was at me, he never neglected his child. Each night, Marcus rubbed my stomach and talked to him. It was usually stuff about how his day went or how happy he was to be his daddy. Sometimes he read a short story. It wasn't anything earth shattering, but it was consistent.

Mrs. Colbert came in earlier and tried to rub my stomach in an effort to calm him, but it wasn't the same. Even in the womb my baby needed his father, and I must admit that his mother did too.

I decided to give Marcus a call. Maybe if the baby could hear his father's voice he would calm down. Marcus usually stayed up late the night before a big presentation so I wasn't really concerned about waking him up. I called but the phone went straight to voice mail. I sent a text asking him to call me as soon as possible and waited.

After about 30 minutes, I began to get concerned. Marcus was pretty good about keeping his phone near and the volume up loud in case I called. He was a pretty light sleeper so the ringing of the phone was all that was needed to wake him. What could he possibly be doing? I wasn't the type to call just to be calling when I knew he had business to handle so he really had no reason to avoid me. *Or did he?* I didn't want to think the worst, but I couldn't help it. I dialed the number to the hotel where Marcus was staying and asked to be connected to his room. Marcus answered on the third ring.

"Hello," he said. He didn't sound the least bit tired.

"Marcus, I called and texted you. Are you okay?"

"You did? I'm sorry. I hadn't noticed. Is something wrong?"

"Yeah. Kinda. Your son won't let me sleep. He's bouncing around in there like he's on a trampoline. I was wondering if you could talk to him. I'm hoping that will calm him down since he's used to you spending time with him every night. We probably should have made a recording of your voice before you left. He's not the only one who misses you."

"You really think that's what wrong?"

"Yeah, I do, but there's only one way to find out. Do you mind?"

"No. I can do that. Put the phone next to your stomach."

Just as I was about to say okay, I distinctly heard someone sneeze. "Marcus, what was that? Is someone there with you?"

Marcus took a deep breath. "I can't do this anymore. We've told enough lies and kept enough secrets. Yes, someone is here."

"Who is it?" I braced myself for what I already knew.

"It's Lisa, but we're not doing anything. We were just talking and she's getting ready to leave."

I wanted to scream. I wanted to cuss. I wanted to cry, but I did none of the above. I wasn't about to go back into labor because my child's father was a low-down conniving cheater.

"Natalie? Natalie? Are you still there? Nat, say something," said Marcus.

I said, "Do you think I'm *that* stupid? I know *you,* Marcus, and you slept with Lisa."

My last words were, "I'm gonna tell your momma" before I hung up the phone.

Chapter 6

Marcus

I would be lying if I was to say that I didn't enjoy the company of Lisa. The softness and moistness of her lips, the firmness of her breasts against my chest, the sweetness of her shoulder blade, and the warmth of her breath against my neck, the feel of her body as I was buried inside the warm folds of her love—were all moments of intimate bliss that I needed and desired.

Love is a fragile thing. It's easy to fall for, yet hard to get rid of. When and *if* I decide to love—I love hard, and I love for real. I was a wounded man. Lisa hurt me. It took me a while to acknowledge it, but she did. I wore that hurt underneath a mask. It was a mask that I could no longer continue to wear.

So, when the opportunity presented itself again on that dreary rainy night in Seattle, fate would reign supreme. Was I wrong? Hell, yeah, I was. I knew it, but so did Lisa. However, like teens in their rebellious years, we broke the rules. Our bond and love never had a code that we couldn't hack. There was no password safe with neither one of us that ultimately would deny ourselves access to that love. Natalie was that password, and Lisa was the hacker that particular night.

Love is patient and love is kind, but most of all—love can fuck your life up. So that's where I am at this moment—back at a fucked-up spot.

By the time Natalie had called that night, Lisa and I were in the midst of saying our good-byes. She was just coming off a cold, and when she sneezed, I knew the jig was up. In a funny kind of way, I was glad she did it. I've always prided myself about being a stand-up guy. So that's why I decided to be honest with Natalie. Well, partially honest. In my mind, I could hear Johnnie Taylor's "Running Out of Lies" song in my head. You know the part when he and his conscience begin to engage in conversation, that's where I was at that moment. I knew it would be hard to think of an alibi.

Honestly, I was relieved yet surprised. I was expecting pain and venom to have been spewed over that phone. However, Natalie remained calm about it. I'm laughing as I think about it now. Did she say she was going to tell my mom? It seemed a little high-schoolish. I just can't seem to get my life on track.

After I got off the phone with Natalie, I reached over to the other side of the bed to grab my shirt. It was resting under Lisa's right thigh. I tugged lightly in an attempt to break it free from her. Our eyes caught each other. We didn't need to say a word. Besides, there was nothing we could have said that would have changed the course of that night. I sensed a little regret on her face. I couldn't decide if it was regret about what we had just done or regret for what could have been. I didn't even bother to ask. Some things should just remain a mystery. Now, sitting at the edge of the bed, Lisa began to stand. I watched as she began to lift a pair of my boxers over her legs before putting on her pants. The pink boy shorts she had worn over here were too moist for her to put back on. She began to fasten her bra. Her breasts were as near to perfection as perfection could get. The rain was still tapping against the hotel's windowpane. She ran her hands over her hair as if they were a comb. She then moisturized her lips with her tongue as she began to fiddle with her keys.

"You know, you don't have to go," I said.

She sighed and sat back down on the bed opposite me. She placed her hand atop mine and squeezed lightly. "I know I don't have to, but I must."

A melting pot of emotions was boiling inside of me. There I was, in a hotel room with a woman I used to . . . *still* love. I have another woman at home pregnant with *my* son that I've grown to have love for. And I have a mother who was going to go upside my head as soon as I got back home. So, when I say that my life is a fucked-up roller coaster—it's a fucked-up roller coaster. Not only was I naked emotionally, I was still naked physically as well. I grabbed my pajama pants that had been flung over the arm of a nearby chair. As I stood I could feel the sleekness of the empty condom wrapper underneath my foot. Now standing, I said, "It's storming too bad. At least let me drive you home and I'll catch a cab back."

"You've always been quite the gentleman, Marcus," she said as her eyes began to well up with tears. Her head dropped, and then almost simultaneously, she raised it back up. She exhaled deeply before she continued, "You have a *son* on the way, Marcus—a son. I was supposed to have your babies."

I sighed. "Yes, this is true. I have a son on the way." At that moment, it became apparently clear that there was no way we would ever be able to fully recapture that perfect moment in time we *once* had. Sure, we could always rekindle a flame, but a flame is meant to burn out over time. What we once had was more like the sun, an everlasting type of fire. It was a fire that we allowed to burn underneath the stillness of the night.

Chapter 7

Natalie

"Can I trust you?" That's the question I asked Marcus when I found out I was pregnant and I was considering an abortion. He told me yes, but it's obvious that was a lie. I can't trust him to do right by me. I can't trust him not to lie. I can't trust him not to sleep with other women, and now I'm wondering if I can trust him to help me raise this child. They say what goes around comes around, and I guess this was my punishment for breaking up Marcus and Chanel. I honestly thought we were going to be okay. I thought if I gave it time, he would grow to love me, but now I see more clearly than ever before. Marcus will never love me the way he loved Lisa or Chanel. The only part of him I would ever truly possess was growing inside my stomach. How one man can make me feel unloved and unwanted to this magnitude is beyond me. What I do know is he doesn't deserve that kind of power.

I cried myself to sleep last night. I cried for myself. I cried for my relationship, and I cried for my unborn child and the two-parent household he would never have. Mrs. Colbert tried her best to console me, but she couldn't. I wanted to blame her. I kept thinking that she and Mr. Colbert had to do something wrong when raising Marcus. He had no sense of loyalty and no compassion. He didn't even try to hide the fact that he cheated on me. He sat there on the phone and boldly and honestly told me that *she* was there. He didn't care that I was at home on complete bed rest because of a difficult pregnancy I was having carrying *his* son. He didn't care that upsetting me could have sent me into labor again. The only person Marcus cared about was *Marcus*. Selfish bastard.

I couldn't even be angry. I was sad and disappointed but not angry. I accepted my role in this. I made a man the center of my universe hoping he would love me, and it backfired. Now here I am lying on my back, looking at the ceiling, wondering how I got to this place. I could feel the puffy swell of my eyes and the dryness that accompanied it. A result of massive amounts of tears.

"Good morning, sweetheart," said Mrs. Colbert. "Are you feeling better? I don't know what has gotten into that son of mine—"

"Mrs. Colbert, could we not talk about Marcus or what happened last night? Right now, the only thing I want to focus on is delivering a healthy baby."

"Of course. I completely understand. What do you want for breakfast?" She rubbed my hair.

"To be alone."

"What?"

I rolled on my side and looked at her. "I don't mean to be rude, but I would like some time to myself. Would you mind going home today?" The sight of her at that moment sickened me. He was an extension of her, and I didn't want him . . . or her anywhere around me.

"Is that safe? Should you be left alone? What if you go into labor again while I'm away?"

"I'll be fine. I have your cell phone number, and at the first sign of trouble, I will call you," I promised.

"I'd rather not leave. I can go in another room and not bother you if you like. I'm concerned about you and the baby." Mrs. Colbert was a short stately woman. Marcus resembled her quite a bit. He had her eyes. She looked tired. I was sure it was a result of being up with me most of the night and worrying about what was to come. She needed to go home and get some rest.

"PLEASE, Mrs. Colbert, I would like to be completely and totally alone—at least for a few hours. You have to understand that this is hard for me. I just found out that the love of my life, the father of my child, slept with his ex-girlfriend with no regard for us, our child, or the life I thought we were building for him. I need a minute."

She nodded her head. "All right, sweetheart. If that's what you want. I'll go run some errands and come back to check on you this afternoon. For what it's worth, I care. I know I'm not your mother, but I like you, Natalie. I'm on your side." She gave me a hug.

"Thank you," I said. She really was a sweet woman. Why did her son have to be such an asshole?

It took Mrs. Colbert about an hour to gather her things and leave. She left me some food by the side of my bed.

As soon as she was gone, I called my brother to come get me. I had texted him early that morning and told him that I no longer wanted to stay in Marcus's home. He and his girlfriend, Patrice, promised to come get me.

Once they arrived, I instructed them about what to pack. After all my things were gathered to my satisfaction, my brother picked me up and carried me to his car and placed me in the backseat. His girlfriend grabbed Pepper and put him in his kennel. He yelped like she was killing him. He hated that thing, but we were going home where we belonged. There was no way I was going to stay somewhere I obviously wasn't wanted.

"I guess one ass whooping wasn't enough to let him know to do right by you. I'm gon' end up killing this fool," said Jessie.

I rubbed my stomach. "You'll do no such thing. I need him to help me raise this boy. Besides, he found his wallet, and I'm trying my best to protect you. But eventually, I'm going to have to tell him that you and Manny beat him up. Don't give him more reasons to press charges against you. Your career is going great. The last thing you need is to end up in jail."

My brother looked at me through the rearview mirror. "You're right, Nat, but how would he like it if someone did his little sister like this? I just want to punch him in the face." He chuckled. "I did that already. I want to punch him in his face, *again*."

"That makes two of us, but let it go. I am. I'm leaving him, and that's the only punishment you or I are going to enact. You feel me?"

"I got you, but that fool is on thin ice."

"I'm here if you need me," said Patrice. "Now that I'm managing Jessie full time, my schedule has a lot more flexibility."

"Thanks. I appreciate you both."

We arrived at my place, and they helped me get settled on the couch and left. The apartment could use a good dusting, but otherwise, it looked just as I left it. As soon as they let Pepper out, he ran around the house sniffing everything as if he was trying to make sure it was just as he left it. He sneezed a couple of times, and then hopped on the couch with me. I had the cable and Internet suspended since I wasn't there. I'd get it started again tomorrow. Jessie had a photoshoot that day and couldn't stay. It was okay. I needed some time to myself. It was nice to be in my own place again. Around 1 p.m., I began receiving phone calls and texts from Mrs. Colbert. She must have returned to the condo and realized that I was gone. I didn't answer. I was in no shape to listen to her fuss or try to convince me to return. They finally stopped after about 2 hours, and then I received a text from Jackson. He said he needed to talk to me and it was urgent. I told him where I was, and he said he was on his way. I realized while I lay there waiting for him that coming home may not have been the brightest idea. I had no way of letting him in once he arrived. I wasn't supposed to move around.

Luckily for me, or perhaps unluckily, my brother left the door unlocked. Jackson entered and sat next to me on the couch. He looked very handsome. He was wearing his favorite suit. It was black. I assumed the red shirt he used to complement it must have been new because I'd never seen it before. He only wore that suit on days that he had an important meeting. He said it brought him good luck. He looked sad, though. I could tell something was seriously bothering him.

"How are you?" he said.

"I'm okay. What about you?"

"I've been better." He took off his jacket and loosened his tie. The white shirt he wore had his initials monogrammed on one of the cuffs. "What I have to say isn't going to make things better, but it's probably better if you know sooner rather than later so that you and Marcus can plan for it."

"There is no more me and Marcus. I'm done. Did he send you over here to check on me?"

"He called, and I know what happened, but I'm not here for him. I'm here for you." He took a deep breath. "My father found out about you and Marcus. How, I don't know. It was probably one of those gossiping heifers at the office. He told me to fire you."

"What? Does he know that I'm home on maternity leave?"

"Yes. But you know as well as I do that we have a strict policy about dating clients unless there was a preexisting relationship. He said that we have to set an example. We have some pretty high-profile and rich clients, and he can't have the staff thinking they can bed them and get away with it. Some might even get pregnant looking for a pay day."

I raised an eyebrow. "He doesn't think that's what I was doing, does he?"

"Of course not. Marcus isn't rich. He makes good money but you'd be stupid to think you hit the financial jackpot with him. I looked out for you though. I talked him into a generous severance package. It should float you for at least 6 months, and we won't officially terminate your employment until after the baby is born so that the birth will be covered under your insurance. After that, I suggest you get Marcus to put him on his insurance."

I was dumbfounded. This couldn't have come at a worst time. I tried to rationalize this out loud. "Okay, I'm pregnant and on total bed rest. My man cheated on me. I am leaving him and just lost my job. This is turning out to be one hell of a day."

It was obvious that Jackson didn't want to do this. He looked so guilty. "I'm sorry. I did everything I could short of threatening to quit if he fired you. Knowing my pops, he would have let me go just to prove a point."

"What point is that?" I said.

"That I work for him, and he is, and forever will be, the head you-know-what in charge."

I laughed. That sounded like the old man. "Don't beat yourself up, Jackson. I'll be okay. Thank you for going to bat for me. The benefits and the severance package are generous. I'm sure I'll be able to find something when I get back on my feet. It will be nice to spend time with my son without having to rush back to work. Besides, now that I'm leaving Marcus, you better believe I'll be asking him for child support. With what he makes, I should get a nice amount. I'll be fine."

He looked at me and smiled. "Marcus is a fool. You are one hell of a woman." He patted my hand. It was warm and reassuring. I welcomed his touch. I needed to know that someone of the male species who wasn't related to Marcus cared.

"A woman who can't seem to hold on to her man," I said. "I'm also not too bright. I came home knowing good and well I need someone to care for me. I can't even empty my own pee pot. What a loser I am."

Jackson looked at the small container I was using to pee in that was now on the floor and half-full of urine. "I see. I'm here now. What do you need besides an empty pee pot?"

"Mrs. Colbert made me some food, and I'm getting hungry. Could you warm it up for me?"

"Sure thing. What else?"

"Nothing. After that, you are free to go."

He took off his tie and rolled up his sleeves. "I'm not going anywhere. Someone has to redeem the reputation of good men everywhere. It might as well be me. It's obvious no one has been here. The place could use a good dusting. I bet you don't even have groceries."

I blew him an imaginary kiss. "Guilty as charged. Thanks, but you don't have to babysit me or clean my place. That's not your job." Tears began to flow from my eyes. "My child's father is supposed to be here, but he's not. Instead, he's in Seattle on a business trip and sleeping with the woman he really wants to be with."

Jackson took his hand and wiped my tears away. "No more tears over him. You've cried enough. Marcus is officially on my shit list. What he did was foul, and I'm going to make sure he knows it. I'm here for as long as you need me."

I sniffed, "Thank you, but I thought you were here only because you had to fire me?"

"No. I'm also here because I'm crazy about Natalie Tellis. I've missed you. Neither the office nor my life have been the same since you left. I've kept my distance out of respect for your wishes and my boy. But I see now, he doesn't deserve you, and under the circumstances, you need me. I'm here. In whatever capacity you need me to be—friend . . . or more than a friend." With that, he got up from the couch and went to the kitchen to warm up my food.

Damn! was all I could think as I watched him walk away. *Maybe I'm not such a loser after all.*

Chapter 8

Marcus

I left Seattle as I came—to the sound of rain. With my eyes closed, I tried to concentrate. I focused on blocking out any and all the *noise* that had been consistent road blocks in my life's journey. As I sat, I attempted to catch an extended moment of clarity. The dysfunction within my love life was beginning to affect my work performance. I've always been the one to effectively maneuver between the two, but as of late, it's been getting the best of me.

My last meeting in Seattle lasted longer than I intended. I was uncharacteristically unprepared and unfocused. I was fumbling over words and forgetting essential details that I would normally breeze through effortlessly. As a result, I missed my initial flight as I had to make sure I left with some respect on my name. I got to the airport, waded through security, found my plane and waited patiently to board. This is actually the first time I've had some alone time since the whole ordeal with Lisa and Natalie. Maybe this is what I needed before I returned to the place that I now consider being the land of the unknown—home.

Sit back and enjoy this, Marcus, is what I kept telling myself. I needed to meditate. I needed to find some comfort within my mind and my heart. I'd been living my life like a black widow. I've been entrapping the emotions of the people I cared about in my web of lies, deceit, and treachery—unintentional, but still wrong.

As I unbuttoned the top two buttons and rolled back the sleeves of the white collar shirt that Natalie had purchased for me online prior to my travel, I could feel the tension inside my shoulders. Flashes of Lisa kept scrolling through my mind. It was obvious that I still had feelings for her. Maybe I hadn't allowed myself enough time to heal. Maybe I shouldn't have engaged in a relationship with either Natalie or Chanel. Sometimes as humans we underestimate the importance and quality of allowing ourselves some *me* time. That *me* time possibly could have been the peace I needed to get over Lisa and eventually could have pushed me to become the man I know I can—correction—the man I *will* be.

My openness and willingness to love *after* lust has been my downfall as of late. My neediness to have the physical presence of a woman at all times is becoming more trouble than the pleasure it brought. Don't get me wrong, I don't lack in confidence or self-esteem. I'm not the one who needs validation from others to determine my self-worth. It's not like that at all. It's more of a normalcy deal with me. I got so spoiled with having Lisa around all the time. When she chose to move rather than stay in Nashville with me, maybe I overreacted by suggesting we end things. Perhaps we could have made a long-distance relationship work. I guess my so-called *lack of constraint* with the ladies is my way of filling that void. The problem is, I've been filling and *feeling* it more than I should.

I haven't always been this way. To be honest, I consider myself to be more of a one-woman type of man. I've always admired the relationships that mirrored my parents. I grew up in a balanced home, where love permeated throughout. That love extended beyond our four walls. That had always been the type of love that I strived toward with the woman of my choosing. That was the type of love that Lisa and I once shared.

They eventually called us to board. I sat in my seat and continued to mull over my situation.

I don't mean to undervalue or disrespect the relationships that I've had with Chanel and my current one with Natalie. The feelings that I've had for them were definitely real, but I'm not sure it was the *real* thing.

Once I arrived in Nashville, I caught a taxi to my condo. During the ride, I decided to call my mother back. She had left me a number of texts and voice mails. Hell, she even logged into my little sister's social media accounts and blasted my inboxes. My mother is something else. She sounded hurt in her messages. I hated the fact that she had to be caught in the middle of my crazy situations.

As soon as she answered the phone, that hurt turned to anger real quick. "Boy, what in the hell has gotten into you?"

She didn't even give me time to respond before she continued. "Don't say a word. Just listen."

My mother's voice carried all the way to the front of the taxi. I knew this by the way the driver kept looking in his rearview mirror snickering with each motherly onslaught.

"I know I raised you better, boy. You just gonna keep on disrespecting your last name, huh?"

I attempted to get a word in again . . . to no avail.

"Shut up and just listen."

I exhaled. There was no need for me to carry a shield to protect myself. I deserved all the verbal jousting that was coming my way.

"You have a son on the way, Marcus—a SON! The life as *you* know it is about to change."

"I understand that, Ma, but—"

"Did I say you could speak? Just listen. That's why you're in all this mess now as it is. You've been acting without thinking or listening to your inner right thing."

"*Inner right thing,* Ma?"

"I know what I said, and why are you still talking? Now, you have a baby on the way and a woman who could make your life a living hell in the flesh if you keep on behaving the way you've been. Son, I don't think you fully understand the wrath that is heading your way. I'm telling you this because I love you. You keep on playing with these girls' hearts and the game will most definitely end with *you* on the losing end. And it will be a loss you may not be able to bounce back from, if you catch my drift."

I continued to listen as my mother vented her frustrations about my actions. I knew she was right, but what was done was done. I couldn't change the past, I could only prepare for a better future. Will that future include Lisa, Chanel, or Natalie? I can't answer that. However, I know it *will* include my son. She let me have it the entire ride. She ended her call with, "You'll see what I mean. It's a cold world out here. You need someone to share your inner world with to keep the chill away."

Needless to say, when I entered my home, I wasn't surprised to find it empty—meaning, no Natalie. However, she definitely left her mark. The smell of orange peel was dominating the kitchen. I could still see the fresh remnants of the delightful fruit on the cutting board. There was a peanut butter and banana smoothie half blended in the blender. Dishes were scattered throughout the kitchen. I had to have a *woosah* moment. If there was anything that irked me more than anything, it was an untidy place. Since Natalie was on bed rest, I assumed it was my mother preparing all her favorite things. She could have at least washed the dishes before she left. There were pots and pans of now spoiled cabbage, black-eyed peas, and what looked like might have been smothered chicken. I could tell because there were still some small pieces of chicken lodged in the cold gravy. The whole scene made my stomach turn.

As I made my way to my bedroom, I heard a knock at the door. I looked at my watch and said to myself, *Who can this be at this hour?* In a voice deeper than usual, with some extra authority, I asked, "Who is it?" No answer. I repeated, "Who is it?" Still, there was no answer.

I must confess that I was still a little on edge after the whole robbery ordeal. There were still questions I needed answers to. Not willing to take any more chances, I grabbed my loaded weapon from underneath my desk and eased toward the door. I didn't have a peephole, so whoever was on the other side would remain a mystery if they remained silent.

Before I knew it, I was slowly unlocking the door. As I opened it, I braced myself for the unexpected. Then I calmed a little. After all, it could have been a number of people on the other side: my mother, Natalie, or my good friend, Jackson. It was none of them.

"Hey, Marcus," the voice on the other side said.

As if my life couldn't get any worse than what it was, nothing surprised me anymore. However, I couldn't do anything but laugh at the irony of it all.

"Why the laugh?" she asked.

"It's nothing. It's been a crazy past couple of days. I would more so call it insanity as opposed to comic relief," I replied.

Noticing the weapon in my hidden hand she said, "Well, it looks like someone has found themselves in more trouble than expected."

"You just can't be too careful anymore," I replied.

"This is true." She pondered her next question before she asked, "May I come in? After you put that thing away, of course."

"Hold that thought" I said and shut the door.

I exhaled, placed my gun back underneath the desk, and contemplated some more before I opened the door and replied, "Sure thing. C'mon in."

Chapter 9

Natalie

I hadn't heard from Marcus in over 24 hours, but I didn't care. I didn't call him, and he didn't call me. I wouldn't have answered if he had. Right now, I hated him. The only thing he had done right was send Jackson to check on me. And he hadn't left my side since he got there except to go to the grocery store. I was grateful for him because I wouldn't have made it through the day or the night without him. I don't know what I was thinking when I allowed my brother to bring me home alone. I knew I wasn't supposed to get up and do anything for myself. Jackson waited on me hand and foot.

I had trouble sleeping. I was restless, and the baby was restless. Neither one of us seemed to be able to find a comfortable position, but only one of us was throwing a fit about it. Jackson tried his best to make it better. He rubbed my stomach and sang to Trenton in his soft tenor tone until he calmed down—although he started right up again about 30 minutes later. I enjoyed the song even if he didn't. I can tell that this little boy is going to be something else. It's obvious that he likes attention. Eventually, he settled down for good, and Jackson and I fell asleep in each other's arms. Pepper snored loudly at our feet.

The next morning, we were both awakened by a loud banging on the door. It sounded like the police. If I were a criminal I would have been worried. Jackson slept in his boxers and stopped to put his pants and shirt on before he went to see who it was. He came back with the weirdest look on his face. He stood in the doorway of my room and said, "You have visitors. An elderly woman who says she's your—"

Before he could finish I heard a woman's voice say, "Get out of my way, son. I don't need no introduction." And in walked my grandmother followed by Manny.

"Grammy!!" I said.

"Yeah, baby. It's me. Sorry it took so long for me to get here, but that gout had me down something serious."

She was a glorious sight to see. I hadn't seen her in almost a year, although I was a little concerned about her timing. I yawned. "What are you doing here?"

"When my grandson calls me and says my only granddaughter needs me, I go where I'm needed. He sent this young man to pick me up. I haven't seen him since he was a boy."

Manny stood there smiling like he'd delivered the best gift in the world.

"Hey, Nat Nat." He came over and gave me a hug.

"Hey, Manny. It's good to see you."

Jackson cleared his throat. I got the hint. "Grammy, this is my friend Jackson. He's been helping me since I came home," I said.

"Friend? You mean this ain't your child's father?" said Grammy.

I shook my head. "No, ma'am. He was actually my boss until I got fired. Now he's made himself my unofficial nurse."

"Oh Lord. This is worse than I thought." She sat down on the edge of the bed. "My granddaughter done screwed her way out of a job. You not sleeping with him too, are you?"

Why would she ask me such a thing? "Grammy!!! Of course not. In my condition, I can barely walk, let alone have sex. My child's father is out of town with another woman. Jackson has been helping care for me."

"Baby, you ain't got to do nothing but lay there," she said with a chuckle. "Yeah, I heard about your child's father from your brother. We'll worry about him later. Young man," she said to Manny, "Help an old woman with her coat."

Manny helped my 80-year-old grandmother take her arms out of the same navy blue wool coat she'd worn since I was a child. There were several small holes in it where it had been gnawed on by moths, but Grammy didn't care. She always said it was her good coat and refused to part with it. Manny slung her coat over his arm and crossed the room to hang it up in my closet.

Grammy then turned her attention to the other man in the room. "Jackson, I took the bus from Detroit, so I'm tired and hungry. Can you cook?"

"Yes, ma'am," he said.

"You can call me Grammy just like everybody else," she said smiling and patting him on the arm.

"Yes, Grammy. I can."

"Well, you and Manny go fix me and my granddaughter some breakfast."

"Excuse me?" said Jackson.

"You heard me, son. My granddaughter says you're here to help, so help. It's morning, and we need breakfast. The baby's got to eat, and so do I. I'm not accustomed to missing no meals." She patted her round stomach underneath her brown skirt and blouse. She wore her coffee-colored support hose and some ugly brown orthopedic shoes. I assumed she needed them because of the gout.

I laughed. That was just like my grandmother . . . running things. She didn't care that he was the head of a successful insurance firm. She didn't care that she didn't know him. Jackson looked at me like he was expecting me to help.

"Don't look at me," I said. "What Grammy says goes. You two better get in the kitchen if you know what's good for you."

Grammy chuckled again. This time her dentures almost slipped out. She never would use anything to keep them in place. "Yep, but before you do, go get me a warm facecloth with a little soap so my grandbaby can wash the sleep out her eyes. You just wakin' up? It's 9 a.m. You shoulda' been up."

"It's not like I have someplace I need to be, Grammy."

"I guess you have a point, Nat, baby."

Jackson laughed and shook his head. "Only because it's you." He went and got a washcloth as instructed, and then he and Manny headed for the kitchen.

My grandmother took off her cream hat and came to the side of the bed. She seemed to have more gray hair than I remembered. It was pulled back into a tight bun. "Let me see you." She pulled back the covers and looked at my massive protruding stomach. She took her hand and rubbed it several times. "This here is going to be a big baby. I hear he keeps trying to come out."

"Yes, ma'am. I was in the hospital for over a month. I'm sorry you had to come all this way. I told Jessie not to bother you. I knew you hadn't been feeling well."

"Nonsense, child. I'm much better now. I would have been here sooner. What I want to know is why you never told me all that was going on with you and this here fella that got you pregnant. Why you want to hold on to a man that's full of such foolishness? We Tellis women are *strong*. We don't need a man to help us raise our children—especially, if he don't want to act right."

My brother has a big mouth! "Grammy, I believe children need both parents. Just because you raised Momma and Uncle Joe by yourself, and Momma raised me and Jessie alone doesn't mean I want to raise my baby without a father. I just had to try."

"You see what it's got you, don't you? Egg on your face. Look around. Do you see that man around here anywhere? Jessie told me he was in Sacramento sleeping with some floosy. Is that true?"

I removed my grandmother's hand from my stomach, pulled the covers back up, and turned on my side. "Jessie talks too much, and it was Seattle," I said.

"Seattle, Sacramento, no matter. What matters is he's up there poking on a woman other than you. You said you *had* to try. You done with him, baby?"

"Yes, ma'am. I'm done. I just want to focus on my child now. He's the most important thing. I really don't want to talk about this, Grammy. I'm tired. I'd rather go back to sleep."

Our conversation was interrupted by another knock at the door.

Grammy yelled out, "You boys keep cooking. I got it!"

Grammy rose off the bed and headed toward the living room. I strained to hear who else was trying to enter my home. I wasn't expecting any visitors. I blinked, and the next thing I knew, Marcus and Mrs. Colbert were standing in my bedroom.

"Now you seen her and you can go," said Grammy coming up behind them.

"Mrs. Tellis—" said Marcus.

"That's right, I'm Mrs. Tellis to you. Everybody else can call me Grammy but not you. You half-inch of a man you have to call me Mrs. Tellis. You are going to give me respect even if you can't respect my granddaughter." Grammy was on the warpath, and if Marcus knew what was good for him, he'd get out of the way.

"Natalie," said Marcus turning his attention to me, "Can we talk? I really have some things I need to say without all these people around."

I turned my head and put up my middle finger. I knew it was childish, but I didn't care. How dare he show up at my home thinking we can talk and smooth things over? I had nothing to say to him. Not yet, anyway.

"You saw that, didn't you? That means no, you cannot," said Grammy. "And what do you mean by *these people*? Natalie and I are the same kind of people. This girl used to fall asleep on my breasts. I'm her blood. If you want to stay here, you will go in the kitchen and cook with the rest of the men. Otherwise, let the door hit cha' where the good Lord split cha'. I wouldn't have even let you in if your mother wasn't wit' cha'!" She sounded like a bad rapper.

Marcus let out an exasperated sigh. "With all due respect, Mrs. Tellis, I need to speak to the mother of my child." He paused as if he suddenly realized what she said. He furrowed his brow, "Rest of the men?"

Grammy poked out her massive breasts and reared back on her heels. "No. What you need to do is keep your little peter pecker in your pants. My granddaughter will talk to you when she wants to, and right now, she doesn't. Now, make yourself useful and go in the kitchen and help Jackson and Manny cook breakfast for me, Natalie, and your mother. Y'all can talk once we've been fed. You hear me?"

She must have noticed the surprised look on Marcus's face when she informed him who was in the kitchen. "What? You think you're the only man that cares about my baby and her baby? Now, gon' in the kitchen with the rest of the men."

Mrs. Colbert had been standing there quietly taking it all in. I was trying to read her expression, but I couldn't, although it was obvious that she wasn't pleased with her son. "Marcus, go. You are really in no position to make demands. I'll stay here with Natalie and Mrs. Tellis and find out what's going on. I'm sure everything will be fine."

"Listen to your mother, *boy*," said Grammy putting lots of emphasis on her last word.

I could tell that Marcus didn't take kindly to being called a boy. As far as I was concerned, he was acting like one. He was a little boy who didn't know how to control his penis.

"Well, now, us women folk can talk and figure out how to fix this so that all parties involved are taken care of, but first and foremost, my great-grandbaby. You know we have to think for men when they've proven that they can't think for themselves."

Mrs. Colbert carefully approached my bed as if she was afraid I was going to give her the finger too. "Natalie, I'm so sorry for my son's behavior," she said. "You would think that he wasn't raised in the house with a man who respected his wife and his children. I know it's not my fault, but for what it's worth, I'm sorry for all the pain my son has caused you. But I really wish you hadn't run off the way you did. Baby, I've been worried sick about you."

"That's real nice. What did you say your name is?" asked Grammy.

"It's Colbert," said Mrs. Colbert.

"We appreciate you apologizing on behalf of your son, but my granddaughter has to accept her part in this."

"What?" I said "What did *I* do?"

"You were spreading your legs for a man that's not your husband. You expecting a man to treat you with respect when you didn't respect yourself. From what Jessie told me, the two of you weren't even a couple, and now you trying to be one for the sake of the baby. Nat Nat, that's not how that works. You 'posed to establish where the relationship is going before you let him in your drawers."

I was going to kill Jessie! How *dare* he discuss my bedroom business with our grandmother! And she was out of line.

"Well, thanks for drawing conclusions based on what my brother had to say. You haven't asked me what happened yet, but I guess that doesn't matter, does it?" I said.

"Don't you sass me, girl. If I'm wrong, you tell me, but you say it respectful like. I'm not too old to tap that tail. I saw a few bushes outside with good switches on them. Now, am I wrong?"

I looked down and played with the edge of my comforter. Here I was, a grown woman in my own home, and I felt like I was 8 years old again waiting to be told to go outside and pick out my own switch. "No, ma'am, you're not, but it's not like I was sleeping with a stranger or someone I didn't love. I love Marcus. I want to have his baby, but I just wish he wanted me too. But, it's obvious he doesn't."

My grandmother came over and rubbed my head. "Chile, ain't no shame in loving a man, but it is some shame in being stupid for him, and you deserve a dunce cap and to be sat in the corner. I know that sounds harsh, but I don't believe in babying grown folks. You got to accept your responsibility for not taking the time to make sure your baby was being brought into this world in that loving home that you say you want. The question is, what happens now?"

I let out a deep breath. She was right, and I knew it. "I'm not sure, but I do know that I no longer want to be in a relationship with him. I can't trust him. No worries, Mrs. Colbert. I have no intention of keeping Marcus or his family away from the baby, but I do need to keep him away from my heart. He's hurt me enough."

"I understand," said Mrs. Colbert. "Under the circumstances, I can't say that I blame you. I commend you for the way that you've held it together."

"I have to. If I get upset, I could go back into labor and there are no doctors or nurses here to stop it. He needs to stay in there for at least another month."

"Don't you worry none. Grammy is here now, and I'm not gon' let anyone upset my baby." She smiled and kissed my cheek. "I love you, Nat Nat. You're going to be a wonderful mother. I know this ain't the way you wanted to bring your baby into the world, but everything is gon' be all right. As long as I got breath in my body, I'll be here to protect you."

"Thanks, Grammy," I said.

Jackson stuck his head in the door. "Excuse me, ladies, but I thought you'd like to know that your feast is almost ready. It looks good too, if I do say so myself. I can't wait to taste some of those crescent rolls we cooked up."

Grammy stood up. "Let me come in there and inspect, but you won't be eating, son. You and Manny are going to leave, and then me, Natalie, Colbert, and her boy are gonna have a come-to-Jesus meeting. We gots to clear the air and get things right."

"Grammy, I would really like Jackson to stay, and I don't want to talk to Marcus. Send him home," I said.

"Listen to me, girl. Jackson is leaving. Why you so attached to him anyway? Are you sure the two of you are just friends?"

Me and my big mouth. I wasn't going to confirm or deny what Jackson was to me, at least not yet. One, because it wasn't anyone's business. Two, I didn't know what he was to me, but I knew I didn't want to be alone, and I didn't want to talk to *that* man.

I could tell that Jackson didn't appreciate being asked to exercise his culinary skills, and then being dismissed. "He's just a friend. Jackson, I'm sorry," I said.

"It's okay. Your grandmother is right. You and Marcus need to go ahead and get this talk out of the way. There is no excuse for his actions. Follow me, Grammy. I think you'll approve of what we have in store for you ladies."

"You're a charming one, aren't you? If I was 40 years younger, you'd have a problem out of me, young man, but I believe you're sweet on my Nat Nat. Y'all don't have to say nothing. I can see it in your faces. I'll mind my own business for now 'cuz you ain't the young man I need to talk to. Let's see what y'all done whipped up for the womenfolk." With that, they both walked out of my room and headed to the kitchen.

"My son is in trouble, isn't he?" said Mrs. Colbert.

"Yep, with a capital T. Once you're on Grammy's shit list, you're in a whole lotta shit. I hope he has some rain boots," I said.

Chapter 10

Marcus

My father always warned me that there would be days like this. He would tell me consistently that there would come a time in every man's life that his boyhood actions would soon define the man he is to become. As the years passed, it was evident that what he had been telling me was the ultimate truth. It's hard for one to imagine that I was listening based on my current situation. Some would assume that I'm currently in what many would define as a "second childhood."

No words could escape my lips that would ease the tension that was at that kitchen table. I could hear the steady tick-tock of the clock that sat above the sink, soon followed by the down-tempo clink and clank of forks scraping plates in conjunction with the slow, yet rhythmic drips from the water faucet. The entire vibe felt like a scene in a movie before the "big bang" dramatic climax.

Feeling uneasy, I attempted to keep my eyes fixated toward the lower region of the table. I could feel their eyes burning a hole through my skin. Beads of sweat began to trickle down my face. The eyes that were watching me were that of Natalie, my mother, and an old woman I didn't know personally, but it was obvious she didn't *like* or *want* me there. I couldn't blame her, but I knew she didn't know the whole story.

Women seemed to be a blessing and a curse to me as of late. I guess that's how the universe works. There is always going to be good omens and bad ones. I sure could use a little help from the universe right now. I need *positive vibes only* at this point.

Breaking the silence my mother said, "Marcus, you need to eat, son. No need to be shy."

"Shy is the last thing he is. He shole wasn't shy when he put his—"

"Grammy!!!" Natalie interjected.

"What? Don't Gram-mee me. It's the truth, ain't it?"

I looked up and caught eyes with my mother. Normally, she wouldn't allow anyone to disrespect me in her presence. However, I read her eyes, and they were telling me that I put myself in this situation.

Suddenly, Natalie jerked and pulled back from the table and placed her hands atop her protruding stomach. Wide-eyed, she squealed with pain. The attention had been removed from me as all eyes became fixated on her. She began to utilize some intense Lamaze breathing techniques she'd learned over the last couple of months. Sweat was rushing from her face, so much so that her hair began to stick to it as if it had been submerged in glue.

My mother was the first to her feet as she was the closest.

"Goodness, child, what is it?" my mother asked.

Natalie's grandmother was slower to her feet, but she was right by her side. She placed her aged hands atop Natalie's. Her pearl bracelet dangled over both hands.

"Breathe, baby—breathe," the old lady said as she placed her dentures back inside her mouth.

I was still sitting. Not because I didn't care or wasn't emotionally attached, but it was as if I was in some type of trance. More words and chaos were surrounding me.

The words became muffled to my ears. I myself began to have hot flashes. My world was caving within my mind. Images of Chanel, Lisa, and Natalie were maneuvering inside my head like a merry-go-round. It was as if I had been punched—knocked out cold and the referee was giving me the 10 count. Both my mother and her grandmother were speaking in my direction, but I couldn't comprehend the meaning. Their faces were just mere blurry images.

Then with clarity I heard the cry and plead from Natalie that no man wants to hear: "Jackson—call Jackson."

It took a couple of seconds for it to register on me. She was calling out to *my* friend as opposed to *me*. It could have been a friendly mistake in her moment of delusion. It could have been the fact that they got close during her time at the office. After all, it was *I* who forced their bond. It was *I* who used Jackson as the mediator of my and Natalie's relationship. Then I began to think some more: why was he here this morning in wrinkled clothing that could have very easily been from the day before? I then remembered the day I was assaulted. There was a cup in his car that looked like Natalie's preferred drink of choice, but I paid it no mind. Before I could complete my mental investigation, I heard the one scream that could snap or wake me from any sleep, trance, or death—my mother's.

"MARCUS—Get your ass up and get me a cool towel."

Now standing on my feet, I did as my mother ordered. I then tried to stand to Natalie's right side to offer my support and concern, but her grandmother nudged me away. She was one mean ol' lady. I decided to stand behind Natalie. I placed my hand atop her left shoulder blade, kneeled down, and whispered in her ear, "Just relax and breathe. Everything is going to be all right. I'm here." I knew I shouldn't have carried her to the table. She was supposed to be on complete bed rest, but she wanted to eat at the table with the rest of us.

She was still breathing fiercely. I then stepped to my left and got in front of my mother and placed my hand upon her stomach. I could feel the little one maneuvering within the walls of her stomach. I began to rub and soothe her belly. It was magic. From the touch of my hand, Trenton stopped for a second. After a while, Natalie's breathing pattern became a little more subdued.

Natalie locked eyes with me as tears streamed down her face.

"Well, I'll be damned," her grandmother said. "I guess he's good for something after all."

"There is strength in a bond—especially from the hand of father," my mother chimed in.

I will admit that the moment got to me. I don't know why it always takes the worst out of a situation to get me to react, but nevertheless, I did.

With my hand still resting on her stomach, Natalie placed her hand atop mine. Her mouth motioned the words "Thank you." I kissed her on top of her forehead.

Our eyes continued to read each other. We knew that more words had to be said as our relationship was still under construction. There were too many questions and not enough answers that stood between us. The only thing that made sense in our world as a unit was the child that she was carrying.

"Grammy, do you mind if we could step in another room and let these two talk?" my mother asked.

Natalie's grandmother looked in Natalie's direction for approval. Natalie nodded.

"Well, I reckon we can."

My mother extended her hand and grabbed Mrs. Tellis's hand and led the way.

As they left the room, I grabbed the cool towel from the table and began to wipe the remaining sweat from Natalie's forehead. She was indeed a beautiful woman. Pregnancy added a special glow to her. However, I never really took the time to consistently notice. This was the stint of our relationship: we would be great, something would happen, we would hate each other, something would happen, and we'd be great again.

Now holding her hand, I asked, "How long are we going to play this game, Natalie?"

She looked away as she replied, "What game, Marcus?"

I held our joined hands in the air as I said, "This game." As I placed them back atop the kitchen table I continued. "We can't continue to do this to each other and to the people around us. It's not healthy—mentally or physically."

I could sense some frustration brewing in her voice as she responded, "That's on you, Marcus—not me. You're the one who went out west to 'work' on something . . . Let me rephrase that. You went to 'do' someone. What? You'd expect that I would just forgive and move on. It doesn't happen that way, and I refuse for it to work that way."

Her grandmother came wobbling back in the kitchen due to the tone and fluctuation in Natalie's voice.

"Is everything all right, baby? Do I need to exit 'that' out the door?" she said while glaring at me.

In my mind I laughed a little. I can't believe that little ol' lady called me a "that" of all things.

"No, Grammy. I'm fine—*we're* fine."

"All right now. Well, I'm in the other room if you need me. I may be old, but my sense of hearing, especially when it comes to trouble, still works like a ho on a stroll."

"GRAMMY!"

As she began to walk back to the other room she replied, "I'm just being honest."

That comedic episode strangely connected me and Natalie back. Not wanting to stir the pot too much, I toned the conversation down some.

"I'm not asking for your forgiveness, Natalie. I own that mistake."

"*Was* it a mistake, Marcus?"

That was the million-dollar question. There was no mistaking that I still had—or have—some feelings for Lisa. That's already been established on more than one occasion. However, I really didn't *plan* on anything like that to happen. At the time, Natalie's and my "relationship" was already on rocky waters. Honestly, we really never officially said we were "boyfriend-girlfriend," "boo-thangs," "man-woman," or whatever title people are using these days. We were what we were—*complicated.* Over time, it was just understood that we were together. We had a child on the way. We saw each other every day, and we were willing to work on creating the best *us* we could for the sake of our child. I tried to be committed.

I guess I didn't try hard enough.

So, I answered her honestly. "Yes. It *was* a mistake. I had no intentions on any of that happening, but it did. It happened, and we must treat it as such."

"So where do we go from here, Marcus?"

"You tell me, Natalie. Where do *you* want it to go from here?"

She remained silent for a second. This was the first time in a great deal of weeks that we decided to have an open and honest conversation without a lot of the emotional fakeness we had been exhibiting over the course of the last 2 to 3 months. At least I had been faking it.

"Do you want *me,* Marcus—as in, me being yours—*exclusively*?"

"Natalie, I will be honest with you."

Her eyes began to well up with tears in anticipation of my answer. I could have easily answered her question with a resounding yes, but what good would that have been long term? I had to spare her feelings, and mine, by being honest.

I continued. "I believe that we're not in a position to do that right now. We have too much baggage between the two of us to honestly and faithfully say that we're ready for that type of relationship. But, I do want to begin to try to build up to that. The first step in trying to accomplish that would be to repair or build our relationship, starting with a solid friendship. Through friendship, trust, and love, everlasting bonds are created."

With teary eyes she nodded. As one tear rolled down her face, she smiled. She placed her other hand atop mine. I placed my right hand atop hers. No words—just silence. We let our body language and energy speak. We listened. Not auditorily, but rather, we listened through the language of our souls. This is where and how foundational connections are cemented—spiritually. Our spirits were not aligned. We were not "soul mates" by the world's definition, so we couldn't, and shouldn't, pretend to be. However, what we *are* is natural beings packed with faults and sin as every other human being in the universe. It was up to us to decide where we would go from here and beyond.

"Well, if we're being honest. I guess we better clear the air then," she said.

Chapter 11

Natalie

The father of my child is a cheater, and he doesn't love me, and I knew it. I once thought we could create a traditional home for our son—one that included a mother and father who loved each other and lived under the same roof. I now seriously doubted that was going to happen. Maybe it was time to let go of my fairy-tale life, but if there was even a sliver of hope for a happily ever after, I had to be perfectly honest with Marcus. I didn't know quite where to begin. I looked around my green and orange kitchen hoping that something would guide me. No luck. I had to just dive in and hope for the best. They say confession is good for the soul. I sure hoped that was true.

"I know you want to know how I got your wallet, but in confessing to you, I have to betray two others which is why I haven't been forthcoming," I said. "I promise you that I didn't have anything to do with your attack, at least not directly. The day I found out about Chanel, I called my brother to vent. I was hurt, and I was angry, and I told him that I wished I could punch you in the face. My brother has always considered himself to be my protector our entire lives, and whenever someone caused me pain, he thought it was his job to retaliate on my behalf. So he and Manny went to your house to teach you a lesson, and when they saw you leave to go for a jog in the park, they decided to do it there and make it look like a robbery."

Marcus didn't respond, but his jaw tightened, and so did his fists. I continued. "They beat you up and took your wallet. Afterward, Jessie called me and told me what they had done. You have to believe me when I tell you that I didn't condone his actions. I was actually quite mad at him for a while. I would never do anything to hurt you intentionally, nor would I ask someone to do it for me. I love you. I've always loved you. I always knew you didn't love me as deeply as I loved you, but I thought in time, if I was good to you, you would. Yet, after your actions in Seattle, I know that what you feel for me is nowhere close to what I feel for you, because I would never sleep with another man."

He looked at me. His eyes held anger. "Natalie, don't try to guilt-trip me. You watched me in a hospital bed with a beat-up face and said nothing about who did it to me."

"Marcus, he's my brother, and Manny is my best friend. When I had no one—when you were busy sexing Chanel and moving on with your life while I'm knocked up with your child—they were there. Then you go and bed another woman while I'm at your house, in your bed, and I can barely move because I'm having difficulty carrying our son. Guess what? I had them then too. Unlike you, I'm loyal!"

I could tell my words cut him, but I didn't care. He had no right to look down on me for anything I'd done.

"Loyal?" He stared at me like I suddenly grew horns on the top of my head. "You almost had my baby without me. You kept me out of the delivery room because I asked a question. You call that *loyalty*? And what about Jackson? It's obvious that something is going on between you two."

I looked down at the table at the bits of uneaten food on my plate. It no longer looked appetizing, but then again, neither did Marcus. I once thought he was one of the most delectable human treats on the planet. Now, he turned my stomach. "I kept you out of the delivery room because you asked a question that got me upset and sent me into early labor . . . *again*. You're selfish, Marcus. Chanel and Lisa were done with no regard of how it would affect me or our ability to coparent our child. How can I be the best mother I can be and work with you if I'm bitter and resentful toward his father? I haven't done anything to deserve the way you've treated me. All I ever tried to do was love you. Jackson has been a good friend. He's been my shoulder to lean on when you couldn't—or wouldn't—be there. I'll admit that he has offered more, but I have refused to accept more than his friendship. If I did that, then I would be doing to him what you're doing to me . . . pretending to care more deeply for him than I do. He deserves better. He's been a great boss, and he's a good man."

I looked up at Marcus with tears streaming from my eyes. "I'm in love with you, Marcus, but I know you're not in love with me. How could you be when you keep offering your heart to everyone *but* me?"

The room grew uncomfortable. Marcus handed me a napkin. I wiped my tears and blew my nose and looked at him.

"I'm sorry, Natalie. I never meant to hurt you. I was just searching for something we didn't have."

"Is there something you want to tell me?" I asked.

He gave me a bewildered look. We already talked about Lisa. What else is there?

I laughed. "Same ole Marcus. Don't confess until asked, 'What was Chanel doing at your house last night?'"

"How do you know that?"

"I guess you forgot that we had a hidden camera installed at the door when I came to live with you. It was so I could tell who was there without getting up. Well, there's an app on my phone that alerts me when anyone approaches and rings the doorbell. Why did she come to see you, and don't try telling me 'nothing.' She's been there at least twice in the past week. What does she want, and don't lie to me?"

Marcus stood up and took a deep breath. "I was hoping we could talk about this later. Under the circumstances, I didn't think you needed any more bombs dropped on you."

I shook my head. "I don't see how you could hurt me anymore than you already have."

He sat back down and reached across the table for my hands. I extended them to him.

"First, let me say that I do love you, Natalie. I think you are a beautiful, intelligent, sexy woman who is going to make a great mother for our child. But we never had that spark, that chemistry, that I had with Lisa or Chanel. And I guess I thought that if that spark wasn't there then what we had wasn't real."

"You're stalling, Marcus. SPIT IT OUT!" I yelled.

"Okay! I'm still trying to process this entire thing myself, but Chanel came by last night to tell me something." He took a long, deep breath and turned his head from me. I knew it must be really bad if he couldn't even look me in the eye. I braced myself for the worst, even though I had no idea what the worst could possibly be.

"She's pregnant, too. She's almost three months along." He turned his head back toward me searching for a reaction, and initially, I had none. I was stunned. I couldn't move. I couldn't speak. Dear God, what did I do to deserve such drama in my life? I never thought in a million years having sex with a man could tear me emotionally to pieces. I looked long and hard at Marcus. He was wearing a red shirt and grey slacks. He had bags under his eyes indicating that he didn't get much sleep. He didn't even bother to comb his hair. I was pretty sure Mrs. Colbert went to his house this morning and made him come over here. I had no sympathy for him. He looked like the devil. If Lucifer had a human form, it was sitting across from me telling me he had a seed growing in another woman the same time he had one growing in me.

He started talking again, but his voice was the last thing I wanted to hear. "I'm sorry. I had no idea. She said initially she wasn't going to tell me and have the baby without my knowledge, but her father told her that I had a right to know."

I was no longer frozen. I wanted to yell, kick, scream, and throw things, but I knew if I did, I could easily go back into labor. I was determined to carry my son to term.

A single tear slid down my already-reddened eyes. "I can't have any part of you to myself, can I? I can't have your heart. I can't have your body. I can't even have the distinction of being the only mother of your child. Thank you for your honesty," I said softly. Then I raised my voice and called out, "Graaaaaaammmmmmy!"

She came in the room, followed by Mrs. Colbert.

"Yes, baby."

"Please see Marcus to the door. It's time to take *'that'* out. You are absolutely right. I don't need a man in my life to take care of this baby. Especially not this one. I'm giving you a gift, Marcus. I'm setting you completely and totally free. You can be with Lisa or your other baby's momma now, or both of them if you want, with no interference or concern from me and how it's going to impact me. I no longer care where you spend your nights or who you stick your body parts in. I don't want you. You are poison. A slow one that eats away at your insides undetected, like a cancer, and by the time you find out, the damage is done. It's too late. Well, the damage stops now. Get out of my life."

Mrs. Colbert stood there bewildered. Her eyes searched me and Marcus for answers, but when neither of us volunteered, she asked. "What other baby's mother? Marcus, what is she talking about?"

Marcus stood up. "We'll talk about it in the car. You don't have to escort me out, Grammy. I know my way to the door," he said.

Mrs. Colbert would not allow herself to be dismissed so easily. "No. We will not talk about it in the car." She looked at me. "You poor, poor child. What has he done now?"

I tried my best to control my emotions. I wanted to be strong, but I couldn't. I held my head in my hands as I sobbed, "Chanel is pregnant, too. You have two grandchildren on the way."

"That bald-headed heifer I met at the hospital?" I nodded my head. Mrs. Colbert then did something none of us expected. She reached up and slapped her only son with all her might. If it were actually possible to slap the taste out of someone's mouth, she did it at that moment.

Marcus's head flew from the right to the left with such force he almost toppled to the floor, but he was able to regain his balance by grabbing the back of the chair in front of him.

Marcus and I were both dumbfounded. Mrs. Colbert usually adored her son. She doted on him, and she certainly wouldn't lay a hand on him—normally. The look on her face held pure anger. The only sound in the room after that slap was the word, "Damn!" followed by hysterical laughter. My grandmother was doubled over on the table laughing as if she had just heard the funniest joke ever told. "Wack'em again. One time ain't enough. Knock some sense into him, girl. That boy has problems. Whack him again!" she said and laughed even harder.

"I don't know where we went wrong with you," said Mrs. Colbert. "When did you develop such disrespect for women? I thought I raised a Christian. Playing with their emotions and having unprotected sex like they're just objects for your personal pleasure. Natalie is a sweet girl, and she's someone's daughter. How would you like it if someone treated your sister the way you're treating her? Leave, son. I can't stand the sight of you right now, and I cannot support such foolishness. I'm so disappointed in you."

She then came to me and held me while I cried. "There, there, child. He doesn't deserve your tears. I'm still here, and I promise you, I'm not going anywhere."

Marcus didn't utter a single word as he left my home holding his reddened and throbbing cheek.

Chapter 12

Marcus

Does love really conquer all, or does time heal all wounds? This is something I've been questioning for the past 2 weeks. Ever since Natalie and I opened up and confessed our wrongs to each other, my feelings have been up and down like Nashville's weather. I was relieved that I was open and honest about the Chanel situation. My conscience was clear when I rested my head at night. However, there were also times when I felt a little on edge, uneasy, restless. This anxiety stemmed from my pursuit of the unknown: not knowing where Natalie and I stood, not knowing if Chanel was really pregnant, and not knowing if I would—or *could*—ever become the man or father I hoped to be.

In times past, I could rely on my mother to be that shoulder to cry on or that ear that would listen. To be honest, I haven't spoken to my mother since she raised her hand to hit me. Was I angry about the ordeal? Yes. Did I deserve it? Yes. Does it take back all the wrong that was done? No. But like I asked before: does love conquer all, or does time heal all wounds?

The weather had been ugly for the past few days. It seemed as if Noah was about to build an ark, and I more than likely would get left off the boat. In one of my failed attempts to meditate, I was startled by a sudden dampness in my upper back area. For a moment I figured it was my heart bleeding outwardly as I was still hurting internally. I turned around and noticed that trickles of water had been seeping through the windowsill. I immediately reached for one of the towels that sat atop the pile of laundry I had been refusing to fold for the past week. At that moment my phone chimed. I had a text.

Bro, it's been awhile. Give me a ring when you get a quick second.

I cringed. I felt a rage begin to build inside me. I was in a state that was as close to a volcano as the human form could mimic. This story line had been playing in the back of my mind for weeks. *How could my so-called brother try to get fresh with a woman I was in a relationship with?* It was my relationship, albeit it wasn't ideal, but it was still *my* relationship. This was one of the primary school rules, the "bro" code, and the line that must never be crossed. Based on Jackson's and my friendship, I, at least, owed him the chance to explain, but the time had to be right—on my terms.

I will be honest and say that some of that rage may have been misdirected. I know part of my rage and anger stemmed from the fact that Natalie played a part in my unfortunate incident that happened at the park. I just kept envisioning her being the puppet master, orchestrating the whole ordeal. Someone could have easily gotten seriously hurt that day. Lives could have been altered forever. Part of me wanted to retaliate. My pride had been challenged. Then I would think rationally and come to the conclusion that the outcome of my retaliation wouldn't be in the best interest of any of the parties involved. This was just something that my pride would have to swallow. No matter how difficult.

Later in the evening, I decided that I would attempt to get back to being me. My mind had been telling me that my moping days were over. It didn't help that I had been watching *Boomerang* religiously lately: the cult classic with Eddie Murphy and that fine Halle Berry. The movie reminded me so much of my situation. I then realized there would never be a happy ending trying to please more than one woman at the same time. Like Eddie's character, Marcus Graham, my intention has always been pure, but somehow, someway, I would always find myself in precarious situations. I begrudged those that had balanced lives: married, kids, white picket fence.

I ended up attending a rally demonstration that was focused on putting an end to police brutality. I was surprised to see a diverse crowd. I was greeted by a young lady who couldn't have been any older than 25. She was standing in her all-black apparel twisting and fiddling with strands of her golden blond hair. She proceeded to smile while she handed me a brochure that had the words, WE WANT JUSTICE, in big bold letters. "Glad you could come."

Looking over the brochure I replied, "Thank you for putting this together." Goldilocks then handed me a sheet of paper and directed me to the right side of the table to fill out a questionnaire.

"So, what organization are you with?" she asked.

"I'm not affiliated with any per se. I just like to stay involved and informed. You know, I just want to do my part."

In her country accent, she replied, "I can understand that. Well, if you're looking to be more involved, don't hesitate to reach out. We need as much help as we can get." She handed me a business card. Her name was Rachel.

Placing her card in my wallet I replied, "So what made a girl like you decide to get into work like this?"

I could tell I had offended her by the question, so I immediately continued. "I didn't mean any disrespect. It's just that I've been in a lot of community functions and the diversity is usually one-sided."

She proceeded to lean over the table. In the position I was standing, I unexpectedly caught a glimpse of her ample cleavage. I immediately fixated my eyes elsewhere.

"You really want to know why and how I got involved?"

I nodded.

She then focused her eyes behind me. She pointed to my left and replied, "It's because of her. She's the reason I got involved. She showed me that injustice is everyone's problem. "

I looked over my shoulder trying to follow where she was pointing. That's when I saw her. She was effortlessly directing and engaging with a crowd of potential key influencers. She walked with a grace and possessed a smile that could light up any room. Goldilocks was still talking, but I didn't hear a word. I slid the questionnaire back to her and said, "I'm sorry, do you mind if I take a seat over there?"

"Sure, but you may have a better view and ability to hear if you sit over there. The speaker system is not that great here."

"It's okay. I'm sure I'll be able to comprehend."

I tried to hurry and complete the sign-in sheet so that I could make my way to the seat of my choice.

"Marcus?"

I sighed internally. Goldilocks had a curious look on her face as she said, "You two know each other?"

"Know each other is an understatement," Chanel said.

I turned. Our eyes caught each other. "Hey, Chanel. How are you?"

Staring directly in my eyes like a drill sergeant, she replied, "I'm fine, Marcus. Thanks for asking. How are you?"

How am I? That was the million-dollar question. This venue wasn't the time nor place for me to *really* expose myself to her. Therefore, I replied with the best answer I could muster, "I'm as good as I can be."

She nodded repeatedly as if she was waiting for me to say more. Chanel looked good, but she also looked tired, like she hadn't been getting much sleep. I hadn't seen her since she showed up at my condo uninvited. She came to deliver her message. I can't say I was the nicest when she did. With everything I was going through my response to the news of her pregnancy could best be described as apathetic. I wasn't happy about it but I wasn't mad about it either. I sat there and listened and assured her I would take care of my responsibilities. I don't know what kind of response she expected but she seemed to be cool with the one she got. Like the true independent woman she was, Chanel let me know whatever I decided she and our child would be fine. She just thought I should know. She gave me a warm hug when she departed and promised to keep me updated. After she left I went straight to bed. I'd had a draining day and all I wanted was rest. Now that I'd had some time to process what she said. I knew we needed to talk some more but I wasn't in any hurry. She was going to be pregnant for a while. Now, with her standing in front of me wearing all black oversized clothing to try to hide her small baby bump I wished I had reacted differently.

"Rachel, can you give us a second?"

"I sure can, girl. Besides, I need to mosey back on over there to get back control of that line."

Chanel then grabbed me by the hand and proceeded to pull me to the side.

"Are you *sure* you're okay, Marcus?"

I sighed. She was the one pregnant and single but she was worried about me. I wondered if the people at her father's church had started gossiping about her yet. She truly was a sweetheart. Chanel was one of the few who could decipher when I was lying. "No, everything is not okay, but it will get there. I can promise you that."

"Don't say the word 'promise,' Marcus—especially not to me."

I broke my eyes away from her. She maneuvered her head in search of them. As they connected once again she continued. "I'm kidding, Marcus. There is no need to be funny around me. I told you—I'm good with it. I'm good with you, Natalie, and you know—*your* baby and *our* baby."

She then flashed the smile that I once fell in love with. Her hair had gotten longer. I noticed she had a couple of strands of gray in the front. My eyes moved toward her belly. I did it unconsciously. As they made their way back up to hers, I said, "I never meant to hurt—"

She cut me off and placed her finger near my lips as she said, "I told you, Marcus. I'm good with it. I mean that. I know this is not the best course of events for you or me. I'm patient. When the time is right, we'll have *that* conversation."

As a man I knew I couldn't wait to have *that* conversation. I understood that patience was a virtue, and I admired the hell out of her for even positioning it that way. However, that was my problem. People had always provided me with comfortable situations. I was never really pushed to own up to my responsibility as it related to relationships. I didn't want the easy way out this time. She may have been good with it, but it was eating me up on the inside. I once prided myself on being in my thirties with no kids. Now I'm about to have two by two different women—at damn near the same time. Enough was enough.

Still holding her hand, I led her toward the door.

Dragging her feet, Chanel said, "Marcus, where are we going? I got to—"

"Are you leaving, Chanel?" Rachel asked.

"Yes. *We're* leaving," I replied.

With a look of anxiety Rachel said, "But . . ."

Before she could finish her statement we were out the door.

Standing under a roof overlay I said, "I can't wait, Chanel. *We* can't wait. Come with me—tonight."

Chapter 13

Natalie

I sat and watched my godmother as she attempted to straighten my room. It was a bit cluttered, and I was in no condition to be walking around trying to put things in their proper place. Proper and in order didn't really seem to have a place in my life as of late. Things between Marcus and me are strained to say the least. I refuse to talk to him, although I will answer his texts. He has asked to see me several times, but I have declined. He stopped by unannounced a couple of times, and I instructed whoever was with me not to open the door. It's not like I'm busy or anything, but I am trying to purge him from my heart and my mind. I can't do that if we're spending time together. Although he was nice enough to make some recordings of him reading that I can play for Trenton. Valentine's Day he sent me gifts and sweet treats. They were thoughtful but meaningless, in my opinion.

It's amazing how his voice soothes our baby when he gets a little too active. If his womb activities are any indication of his career, he's got an excellent future in the NFL as a kicker, or maybe he's using his fists. If that's the case, he's going to be a boxer. I've only got a few more weeks until delivery time, and I can't wait to meet him although I'm dreading having to spend large amounts of time with Marcus. I have no intentions of keeping him from his child. He can come over here and spend as much time with him as he likes.

I'll just have to put my feelings on the back burner and deal with it. I don't hate Marcus, but I do really dislike him right now.

Adina held up a baby-blue nightgown that Pepper had been using for a bed the last couple of nights instead of getting in that expensive, overly cushioned thing I bought for him online. "Dirty or clean?"

"Definitely dirty," I said. She put it in the hamper.

"How did this get on the floor anyway? You're in bed all day."

"I probably changed and threw it over there," I said.

My family and friends have been a huge help. Grammy and Mrs. Colbert seemed to be coparenting me in the absence of my mother. Mrs. Colbert's excessive need to try to make me feel better to make up for Marcus's actions is a little overwhelming at times, but I know she means well.

Even Mr. Colbert has started to take more of an interest in my pregnancy. Previously, he left that to his wife. Now, he calls me at least twice a week. He has assured me that there is a Colbert man who has my interests at heart and cares about my well-being. I can tell he's very disappointed in his son's actions. I get the feeling that their relationship isn't the best right now, but I don't ask. Whenever we talk, the last thing I want to talk about is Marcus. I don't see much of his sister.

Mia seems to be enjoying the newfound freedom that using my car is providing her. She sends me a text every now and then. It wouldn't kill her to pick up the phone and call. Jessie and Manny stop by often to check on me. Well, Jessie does whenever he's in town, but he calls every day. Patrice pops her head in from time to time as well. Adina comes on the days she doesn't have to go to her practice. Today is one of those days. Grammy went home for a few days to "check on her house," but she promised to be back soon. We probably needed a break from each other. God knows I love my grandmother, but she has no filter, and she feels her age gives her permission to unleash her opinions whenever she feels like it. I had grown quite tired of her Marcus bashing. I think that's her way of trying to make me love him less. It's not working. My opinion of him has decreased, but not my love for him.

Adina came to my bedside and fluffed my pillows for me. "So how are you feeling about your child having a brother or sister? Have you thought about if you are going allow them to have a relationship?" she asked. I loved my godmother. She had such a sweet, caring demeanor. I also appreciated how she could give advice without being judgmental. She and my mother had been best friends in college. She often told me how I reminded her of my mom.

I sighed. "I haven't thought that far ahead. Besides, it will be Marcus's responsibility to do that, not mine. I won't stand in the way. However, I don't plan on dropping Trenton over at Chanel's house for play dates or anything. That woman is the last person I want to see. I feel like she took something from me. I thought Marcus and I would get to share the parenting experience together exclusively. I guess the joke's on me."

"I understand," she said while smoothing the top of my hair back. Most days I wear a ponytail, but the hairs are generally out of place from where I rested my head on the pillows and mattress. I often fluctuate between the two in an effort to find a comfortable position.

"I knew," she said.

I looked at her curiously. "Knew what?"

"I knew Chanel was pregnant. I'm her primary care physician. I figured out she was the Chanel you were talking about when I gave her the results of her pregnancy test. She broke down crying and told me the whole story. She really thought that she and Marcus had a chance together. She also admitted that dating her bestfriend's ex-boyfriend knowing he had a baby on the way with another woman wasn't the wisest decision. I wanted to tell you, but because of HIPPA regulations, I couldn't."

"It's okay," I said. "I probably wouldn't have told me either. I'm glad that I found out sooner rather than later, though. I'd hated to have bumped into her at the grocery store or the mall and we're both holding kids that look like him. I can prepare myself for the BS now. I should have known she would be back in some form or another. Nothing about this entire ordeal has ended easily."

Adina grabbed a brush off the nightstand and brushed my edges back in place. "Is it truly over between you and Marcus? Are you really done with him?"

"Hell, yeah! I can only take so much. He is so disrespectful, and if I accept that behavior in the beginning, he's only going to do something worse later . . . although I don't know what that could be short of screwing you or Grammy. The only thing he can do for me is take care of his kid. And you just wait until he's born. I'm going straight downtown to sign him up for child support. I'm sure he'll try to make some arrangement with me, but I'm going to make sure I get every single dime I'm owed."

"Well, what about Jackson?"

"Jackson and I are just friends. He's a great guy, and maybe if we had dated first, it would be different. I'm mad at Marcus, but not mad enough to get back at him by being with his boy. It's hard though. Jackson is an absolute sweetheart. Anything I think I need he gets it. If Grammy hadn't scared him away, he would have come to check on me every day. We talk every day, though, and sometimes, we video conference," I chuckled. "Grammy's so anti-man it's ridiculous. My granddaddy must have really done a number on her. She keeps telling me how I can do this myself, but she does have a point. Me jumping from one man to another wouldn't be good for me or my baby."

I heard someone at the front door. "I wonder who that could be," I said. "If it's Marcus do not let him in."

She smiled. "It's Jackson. I have to go, and I called and asked him to handle the next shift." She put the brush down and got up to go let him in.

The Colberts and my family and friends were taking shifts sitting with me to make sure I was never completely alone. It felt good to know that so many people cared about me. She and Jackson entered my room a few minutes later.

"I hate I have to leave, but my office administrator called and said there was a matter brewing that I need to handle today. Thanks for helping me out in a pinch, Jackson." She gave him a hug.

"No need to thank me for helping out a friend. I'm glad you called." He smiled at me.

I'd grown to love his smile. Jackson really was a great guy, but it scared me that he seemed to be falling for me—hard. I wasn't going to be much company today. I was tired and needed some rest. It amazed me how tired

I felt even though all I do is lie in bed all day. Being on bed rest is quite boring. When I'm not sleeping or eating, I watch TV, listen to music, read, or trade stock options online.

Adina gave me a hug. "Call me if you need me, but I'm sure you're in good hands," she said before she leaned over and kissed my cheek.

"The best," said Jackson.

She then headed for the door. I really wished Adina had let me know he was coming. I was wearing a slightly sheer nightgown. My breasts had grown considerably during my pregnancy. They felt heavy and swollen as my mammary glands prepared themselves to feed my baby. The covers were below my breasts. You could clearly see my enlarged areolas through the fabric, and Jackson noticed. His eyes traveled from my face and settled on my chest. He licked his lips and smiled. I moved my sheet upward to cover myself.

He came over and gave me a peck on the lips. Instead of backing up afterward, he allowed his lips to hover over mine and said. "I missed you. Your Grammy has been cock blocking. She makes it so uncomfortable for me to visit that I stay away," he said with a slight chuckle.

His breath smelled like spearmint gum, and I could distinctly smell the fragrance Kenneth Cole Black emanating from his body. It—and he—smelled nice. "I know," I said. "Please forgive her. She doesn't want me to keep getting hurt. She thinks you're a good guy, though. Grammy just doesn't think it's a good idea for you to be here."

"You know I would never hurt you, right?"

"I know you would never hurt me intentionally." I wasn't up for this conversation. Thanks to Marcus I was emotionally drained, and thanks to a high-risk pregnancy, I was physically fatigued. I'm going to take a nap now. "Do you mind turning off the lights?"

"No. Do you mind if I join you? I've had a long day. I could use some shut-eye myself."

"Sure," I said. I was grateful that he didn't try to continue to have a conversation about us. I scooted over and made room for him beside me in the bed. Jackson had slept in the bed with me before. He was always respectful, so I didn't mind. It was kind of comforting to have him there since Marcus couldn't be. There I go thinking about Marcus again. I really wish I could get him out of my mind. I know he isn't even thinking about me. He's probably somewhere with Chanel. I knew that it was probable that they would get back together. With me out of the picture and their baby on the way, there was no reason for them not to. That would be another situation I would have to deal with when the time came. Sometimes I wished I didn't have morals. It would be so easy for me to just let Jackson become my place of refuge and give Marcus a taste of his own medicine in the process. I'm sure if I let him, Jackson would try to make me forget all about Marcus. I wondered if he was using me to forget about his ex and the children they would never have. It had been less than a year since they parted ways.

He cut off the lights, and I watched him take off everything but his boxers, T-shirt, and socks in the remaining light that streamed from in between the blinds. He really did have a nice physique. He was taller and leaner than Marcus, but the muscles he had were pretty defined.

He then got to the bed, snuggled his body next to mine, and draped his long arm over me. We lay there quietly. I tried to go to sleep, but I was so uncomfortable. I was always uncomfortable. Then I realized that Jackson's penis was poking me in my leg. How could I in my present state give him an erection? I looked like a beached whale, and that made me uncomfortable and insecure.

"Jackson, I think you should go sleep on the coach," I said.

"Why? Did I do something wrong?"

"No, but I'm uncomfortable, and I think it's best if I sleep alone."

"Is there something I can do to help?"

"Yes. I mean no."

"Baby, what's wrong? Just tell me."

I decided to be honest with him. "I don't know what's wrong with me, but for the last 3 days I've been horny as hell. It's the craziest thing. I can't even have sex in my current state, but my hormones are raging," I said with some slight embarrassment. However, Jackson and I joked about sex so much when I was working with him, it wasn't an *uncomfortable* conversation to have. It was always fun and games between us.

He laughed. "Really? I may be able to help with that." He scooted toward my face and kissed me.

"What are you doing?" I said as our lips slowly separated. A slow and appealing moan escaped my lips.

He gave me a mischievous grin. "It sounds like you need a good orgasm, and there are ways to do that without having intercourse."

I put up my hands to stop him from doing whatever he had in mind. "No, that wasn't what I was suggesting."

"Listen, I told you I was here in any capacity you need me. You need to rest. I can help you release that tension so you and the baby can sleep peacefully tonight. I know how you feel about us. There are no strings attached to this, and pleasuring you would bring me great pleasure," he said seductively. He then took his hands and laid them atop my swollen abdomen. "Trust me."

"I do trust you but—"

He put his index finger on my lips to silence me. "Give me 2 minutes and if you don't like what I'm doing, I'll stop."

I was torn, but I was also tried of feeling sexually frustrated every day. I was afraid to use my vibrator because I didn't want to give my baby cerebral palsy or epilepsy or brain damage. I had no idea what all that motion could do to him.

He put his hands on my breasts and started playing with my nipples.

"I don't think this is a good idea, Jackson."

He ignored my words, lowered his head, and he began sucking on my nipples through the sheer fabric of my gown. My body grew aroused, my nipples hardened, and desire started to form in between my legs.

"Hush. I . . . got . . . you. Two . . . minutes," he said in between soft pulls. First the right, and then the left.

I had to admit, his mouth felt good against one of my most sensitive spots. Marcus hadn't touched me in weeks, and my body was hungry for some attention. I closed my eyes and against my better judgment I let him continue. A soft moan escaped my lips. He took that as confirmation to continue. His hands began to roam my body. I felt him pull my gown up around my hips. My womanhood grew warmer. He moved his body downward, he bit me softly on the right inner thigh, and then the left before he flicked his tongue up down and around his target. It felt rough like it had little bumps on it. I never noticed that before. Did he have big taste buds or something?

Without warning, his fingers entered my slick sex. Another moan escaped my mouth. *What are we doing?*

"Oh, Natalie, you feel so warm and wet," he said. "I would love to be inside you, but I know you can't."

He pulled the covers down below my feet and maneuvered his body below mine some more. With his face buried in my love oven I felt his tongue go places it shouldn't go and do things it shouldn't be doing. I lay there and tried to tell myself it was okay. He was just helping me out in my time of need. I really was tense and could use a good orgasm. It felt all right, but I'd had better . . . much better. My eyes traveled to the stuffed bear Marcus gave me for Valentine's Day. It said I love you on its belly. That was a laugh. The chocolate that came with it had been consumed a long time ago and the roses had died. Just like our relationship. Jackson lifted my leg to allow himself better access. He was fumbling and awkward. His licks had no type of rhythm or fluidity. They were jerky and all over the place. I really wanted to tell him to stop and leave this job to the pros, but I didn't want to hurt his feelings. He eventually seemed to find a flow that worked for him *and* me. His efforts began to feel better. After several minutes, I felt a familiar sensation building inside me. Once it reached its pinnacle, I released it and a scream escaped my mouth. My body shook and like he predicted, that tension I had penned up inside me seeped away.

He let out a chuckle. "See? Don't you feel better?" He wiped his mouth on my 1,800 thread count Egyptian cotton sheets before returning himself to the head of the bed. He resumed his place behind me and kissed the nape of my neck. He played with my nipples through the fabric of my gown that was now damp from his earlier exploration.

"I think I'm in love with you, Natalie," he said. "You really should give some thought about us being more than friends. I know you're not over Marcus yet, but I can't stand the way he treats you. I would like to love away any hurt or pain he's caused you. He doesn't deserve you. If I had known he was this bad of a guy I never would have introduced you two."

I now felt even worse. While he was lying there professing his love for me, I was thinking, *He's no Marcus Colbert.* He would have had me where I needed to be in 5 minutes or less, and I would have been screaming to the high heavens repeatedly. He was a professional when it came to anything sexual. Besides, I was in love with him. I truly wanted to stop this incessant need I had to love him, but my feelings for him weren't some light switch that I could flick on and off. I knew Jackson meant well. He was probably right about being a better man for me, but my heart yearned for another man.

"Thanks. Get some sleep, Jackson," was all I said before drifting off to la-la land. I dreamed about Marcus making love to me. It was much better than the reality I just experienced.

Chapter 14

Marcus

Some would use the following adjectives to define the silence that was within the four walls of my home: peaceful, comforting, echoing. However, if those same people only knew the reasons behind the silence, then they would understand and know that it was uncomfortable, painful, and agonizing. My reluctance to become a product of my mind has been a battle I've been fighting for the past couple of months. It would have been easy for me to just succumb to the pressure and continue the useless, self-inflicted, "woe is me" mental beat-down I'd been giving myself during that time, but I was aware that *that* type of thought process wouldn't solve anything.

In times such as this, there are two coping mechanisms that I usually turn to as a means to mitigate the misery: Marvin and bourbon. Marvin and bourbon had become major staples in my household growing up. The soulful and hypnotic hymns that Marvin Gaye blessed my family with would bleed through the speakers at every family function or activity such as Saturday morning cleaning day. The thing about Marvin was that he had a song for any season of feelings that you may have been going through at that time: sad, happy, glad, or mad. I was currently in a season of "the blues," but I knew Marvin would help guide me through it. As Marvin poured his soul into "Anna's Song," I poured myself another glass of bourbon.

The soothing sound that the liquid pleasure made as it found its way to the bottom of the glass was also music to my ears. I used to see my father do this routinely at the beginning of every month, holiday, or times when he was asked to come home unexpectedly from a job.

As I lay comfortably on the love seat, I closed my eyes. My mind began to take a trip down memory lane. I saw flashes of both Chanel and Natalie. That eerie feeling of guilt and uncertainty began to kick back in. The guilt was self-explanatory. The uncertainty was built on the notion of me having to provide and care for *four* more people other than myself: Natalie *and* Chanel in addition to the *two* babies that were on the way.

I still didn't know how to feel about the Chanel situation. I was having trouble finding a way to become emotionally attached. It was all coming too fast—too new, too surreal. It was true enough that I *did* have strong feelings for Chanel, but for some reason, I couldn't transfer those feelings to the pregnancy. I had invested so much time emotionally in Natalie and *our* situation, I wasn't sure I could do it all over again with another person. However, it was no longer an option. I had to, and I had to do it quick.

There was only one person that I was willing to open myself up to and, in return, be receptive of the critical feedback, and that person was my father. However, we haven't been on the best of speaking terms due to my sexcapades and immaturity. But, I knew that when I decided to extend my hand for help, he wouldn't pull back; instead, he would embrace it and pull me in.

We decided to meet at one of his new vices, a cigar bar. My mother calls it *his midlife crisis kicking in*, but as a man, I understood it as a place of peace and tranquility. I arrived at a time *I* perceived to be early, but lo and behold, my father was already there. He was sitting, smoking, sipping, and talking to a woman who looked young enough to be his daughter. It didn't seem like an intimate conversation, but rather innocent. Nevertheless, I had to pull his chain—tease him a little.

"Old dog trying to learn new tricks?"

My father looked at me slightly embarrassed but ready to fire back a not-so-pleasant response—all in fun, of course. "Abby, here is the asshole of a son I was just speaking about."

He smiled and proceeded to shake my hand. In that moment of father and son bonding, I turned my attention to the young lady sitting next to my dad. She was an attractive woman. If I had to guess, she looked as if she was in her early to mid-30s. With her legs crossed, skirt pulled back, just far enough for me to get a glimpse of her long, smooth, toned legs, she extended her hand as she said, "Nice to meet you, Marcus."

"My pleasure," I responded before continuing. "So, Abby is a name I don't hear often in our community."

She smiled as she took a sip of her fruit-infused drink. "I guess that's your way of saying that I have a *white* girl's name."

"Don't take it the wrong way, I was just—"

"No offense taken. I get that a lot. You're right, there's not a lot of sistas named Abby, but then again—I guess that's what makes me unique. Besides—a name is just a name. It doesn't define you, especially as it relates to ethnicity."

"So do you come around here a lot?" I asked in an amateur attempt at probing and changing the conversation.

"Every now and then. Not *too* often though."

I then turned my attention back toward my father as I said, "So, how do you know this old man?"

She smiled as she replied, "I just met this *mature* man today. He was ever so kind to return my cell phone that I must have dropped up front when I was looking for my wallet."

My dad was looking at me with a smile on his face as if he was proud of his act of kindness.

"Well, that sounds like my pops. How did the conversation take a turn about the *asshole*?" I asked.

They both laughed.

"It was just through general conversation. He was telling me—sorry, *Mr. Colbert* was telling me about how *you* always leave your cell phone lying around."

"Yeah, this boy here will forget his own name—on a *good* day," my dad said with a slight chuckle as he took a pull from his cigar.

"Well, don't let me interrupt this male bonding. It was a pleasure meeting you both. Thanks again, sir, for bringing me this phone. It's my lifeline, you know."

"Not a problem at all, young lady. That's what we're on this earth to do—delegate good deeds."

My father was looking directly at me when he made his last statement. Was he saying that I haven't been producing good deeds? I knew he was setting me up for an angle, I just didn't know how. But, I knew I wouldn't have to wait long.

I pulled up the now empty seat next to my dad and picked up the drink menu. Clouds of heavy cigar smoke began to maneuver from my peripheral to my direct view. I wasn't a smoker, so the smoke made my throat tingle as I proceeded to slightly cough.

"Don't tell me you're one of those," my father said.

Still clearing my throat, I responded, "One of what?"

"Sensitive nonsmokers."

"It's not that. It just caught me by surprise," I lied.

"So what's all this mess you've gotten yourself into? You know your mother has been all up and down my ass about your craziness. As if I could have stopped it or fix it."

"I apologize about that, Pop. I'm still trying to make sense of it all my damn self."

"Well, you don't have a lot of time to *try* to make sense of it—you need to buckle down and face your situation head-on. That girl, Natalie, is a couple of weeks away from giving birth to *your* child."

"I don't know how to do it, Pop. I mean—when Natalie got pregnant, that wasn't as big of an ordeal. I felt like—you know—it was something we could handle. But when I got the news about Chanel, it was like a different type of feeling. It was—"

"Call it what it is, son—you're scared. There is no shame in that. Not only are you scared, but you're embarrassed, ashamed, upset, hurt, and confused." He dropped the heavy ashes in a nearby tray before he continued. "All of those adjectives I just mentioned—those young ladies whose hearts and bodies you've been playing with without condoms—are feeling that—times 10."

I sat in silence, soaking in every last word my father had just said.

Breaking the silence, he said, "Listen son, it's not always *what* you do, but *how* you move forward."

"I know, Pop. How would you—"

"Don't wish that shit on me, son," he responded with a laugh. "Trust me, I've had my ups, downs, and all there is in between, but I've never been in this Venus flytrap you've found yourself in. Now your *grandfather*, if he was still here, that would have been the man to talk to. Hell, that rolling stone had 11 kids between *three* women."

I shook my head just imaging the agony he must have been going through.

"Those were different times though, Pop. It was the norm to *spread* the love around."

"Well, the difference is, son—*your* generation makes the baby and spilt. At least *my* generation and the one before it man'd up to their responsibilities—*most* of the time."

"I'm not trying to run from it, Pop. I plan on handling my business as a man and my newfound responsibilities. My issue is just trying to balance it all. Chanel and I just recently had a real heart-to-heart conversation. Nevertheless, I'm still in that, where do I go from here phase."

"Son, you remember when you first went off to school and you were struggling with your studies? You kept whining and complaining that you couldn't balance both studying and working. You remember that?"

"Yeah, Pop—how can I forget?"

"What did I tell you all the way back then?"

"You told me to slow it down, breathe, and trust the process."

"Exactly! That's what you need to do in this situation . . . as hard as it seems like it may be. No matter how you disappointed your mother, me, yourself, *and* those young ladies—at the end of the day, *you* still have the ability to make things right or at least better. Just slow it down, breathe, and trust the process."

I sat in silence. My father finished off the last of his cigar.

"Pop, can I ask you a question?"

As he smashed his nub of a cigar into the ashtray, he replied, "Fire away."

"Have you ever stepped out on Moms?"

My father looked a little perplexed by my question.

"I can't believe you had the audacity to ask me that." He patted me on the back and continued. "Good for you. Tough men ask tough questions. As for your answer—no—I've never cheated on your mother, disrespected your mother, or mistreated your mother. That woman is my world. I can't foresee why any human would *want* to do anything negative to that mother of yours."

"I hope to find that type of love and happiness one day."

"You can, and you will, son. But it first starts here." He pushed his index finger into my chest. "It starts with you. Once you learn to love who *you* are and learn how to forgive *yourself*, all the other great things life has to offer will find its way to you."

Just when I was about to ask him another question, his phone rang. He stepped away to answer. When he returned he told me he had to run.

"What is it, Pop?"

"It was your mother. She's all stressed over your sister; something about her leaving school early today. She thinks she's hot stuff now that she's a senior with wheels. Now I got to get home to take care of some more mess. I swear you kids are messing up my happy time. I thought when y'all got grown I could relax and enjoy life and your mother in peace, but you knuckleheads just don't want to let that be."

"Is everything all right? Do you need me to come as well?"

"You just stay put. You know your mother is still very upset with you. I'll let you know as soon as I dig more into it. Just remember what we discussed."

I watched as my father walked away. I sat alone by the bar for the next couple of minutes. I knew my father was right. I was having trouble showing love and care for anyone else because I still hadn't forgiven myself. When I left that cigar bar, I knew *what* I needed to do, and I didn't want to waste another minute.

I left the cigar bar en route to Natalie's place. While driving, I noticed a car on the side of the road with a flat. I really didn't want to stop and be a Good Samaritan. I was skeptical when the thought initially crossed my mind. I immediately thought about an episode of one of those crazy crime shows I'd watched over the weekend, where a Good Samaritan ended up being the victim in a setup robbery. However, I went with my gut instinct and proceeded to pull over.

When I stepped out of the car, I braced myself for the force Mother Nature was about to send my way. It was still raining heavily, each drop dancing upon my skull before trickling down my face. As I approached the Lincoln Continental, I hesitated a little before nearing the passenger-side window. When I was about to knock, the window slowly rolled down just low enough for one to be able to hear, but also high enough for protection from a stranger in addition to preventing the rain from getting the insides wet.

On the other side of the window was a stubby woman with the most beautiful head of gray hair I'd ever seen. She had little freckles covering her cheeks with stubby hands that seemed to be too swollen for the rings she was wearing. As she tilted her head and peered over her glasses, she asked, "How can we help you?" It caught me by surprise. There I was, standing on the outside in a storm, and she was asking me if *I* needed help!

"Ma'am, I saw that your tire was flat, and I wanted to offer my assistance." She looked over at her husband and mumbled something under her breath. Next thing I know, the driver's side door flew open, a rather short man appeared with an umbrella and cane in hand. He introduced himself and we battled the rain together.

At first glance, he reminded me of my late grandfather. He still had a head full of black hair, but the gray had begun to spread across the edges of his head and beard. He pointed his cane toward the trunk. "In here—I think I have a spare." As he made that statement, I noticed the umbrella shaking as he kept reclutching his hand.

"Arthritis?" I asked.

"Rheumatoid. How did you know?"

"My grandfather used to have it. He walked the same as you, and when I saw you clutching your hands—I assumed."

I had heard that rain could potentially make the swelling worse. As I attempted to wipe some of the rain from my face and eyes, I said, "You can wait in the car if you need to. I think I can take it from here."

Still holding the umbrella over my head as I attempted to jack the car up, he replied, "Young man—nothing would please me more than to help you. Let's just say, when I get back in *this* car, this would have been the manliest thing I've been able to do for quite some time—if you catch my drift."

I caught it, and it made me laugh. There stood a man who was withstanding the pain and agony caused by the rain only to impress a woman whom he's been with the majority of his life, I assumed. I wanted someone to grow old with and someone who loved me enough to stay when I become a fraction of the man I once was. The crazy thing is I have three women who want the job and my dumb ass keeps running them away.

He continued talking. "Besides, I can't allow another man to do *my* job. Why the hell you think we've been sitting here all this time? You're just the lucky one. I turned down about three of y'all before *you* came."

Caught up in the humor of it all, I asked, "Why is that?"

"A man must know when he's been defeated. I knew full well I couldn't change that damn tire when I turned them down and the damn roadside assistance is more than 45 minutes away. So you walked up and I said to hell with it—I'll let him change the tire, but I damn shole won't let him do it alone."

We shared a laugh as if we were old friends. I was indeed the lucky one. Despite the new outfit that I had just purchased not too long ago being ruined by the mixture of rain, dirt, oil, and other residue, I enjoyed the brief but odd conversation. When I finished I made sure to let his lady know that he was "all" man putting that tire on, and I was just there to help. He winked at me, and I waved them off good-bye.

When I got back in my car, I turned the heat on to help dry up some of the rain. I reached in the backseat as I still had some old clothes I had worn earlier in the week helping build a fence with Habitat for Humanity. I thought helping others would make me feel better. It didn't, until today. I decided to put them on. Despite how rough I looked, I proceeded to head to Natalie's.

Chapter 15

Natalie

I awoke to someone standing over me calling my name and gently shaking my shoulder.

"Natalie. Natalie. Wake up—we need to talk."

I drowsily responded with an "Okay" and willed my eyes to focus on the person in front of me in the dim lighting. It was daylight when I went to sleep, but it was obvious the sun had set. The only light in the room was coming from the hallway, and a small sliver of light could be seen underneath the bathroom door.

"Marcus?" I wondered if I was dreaming.

"Yeah. I know I'm not your favorite person right now, but, Natalie, we need to talk."

We then heard the toilet flush. A second later, the bathroom door opened, light flooded the room, and Jackson emerged. "I don't think she wants to talk to you, bro," he said. He looked angrily at Marcus as if he had entered his home without permission instead of mine. He was still dressed in only his boxers and socks. I looked at the clock on my nightstand and realized it was a little after 8 p.m. Our nap lasted longer than I intended.

Marcus looked at him, and then back at me as if searching my eyes for answers.

"Natalie, are you two sleeping together?"

I laughed. "Are you serious? I can't have sex with anyone in this state. We were just taking a nap."

It was ironic that only a few hours earlier I was wishing Marcus was there to make me feel like a woman in the areas where Jackson was deficient, and now, there he was, standing in my bedroom. He didn't look good. His hair and clothes were disheveled. He wore a blue T-shirt, jeans, and dingy tennis shoes that had seen much better days. The stubbly beard on his face indicated that he hadn't shaved recently. He barely resembled the clean-shaven, debonair man I'd fallen for a year ago.

"How did you get in here?" I asked.

"I guess you forgot that I have a key. The only reason I hadn't used it is because I was trying to respect your wishes and stay away, but I can't anymore. You're due any day now, and we should be communicating."

He was right, and I knew it. Jackson was standing behind him as if he were waiting for me to give him the okay to kick Marcus out.

"Jackson, do you mind giving us some privacy so we can talk?" I said.

"Sure. I'll go in the kitchen and fix *us* something to eat."

"No, I mean leave the apartment. I appreciate you coming, but it's time that Marcus and I talk. Our child will be here soon. I think it would be best if we did it in complete privacy."

He looked a little hurt. "Do you want me to come back?"

Up until this point Marcus had barely even looked at him. "That won't be necessary," he said. "I'll stay here as long as she needs me to. Your services are no longer needed. We will discuss this later, *bro*," Marcus said with a snarl.

I sat up in the bed and turned the lamp on the nightstand next to me. The stench of testosterone was strong. I needed some of it gone before I became ill.

"I'll be okay," I said. "If I need you, I'll call." I gave him a reassuring smile. I really did appreciate the way he looked out for me, but at times, he could be a little overprotective. He reminded me of Jessie.

"Okay. Don't let him upset you. I'd hate for you to go into labor," said Jackson, and then put on his pants, shirt, and shoes. He grabbed his tie and jacket from a nearby chair. Marcus turned his head as if the sight of seeing a man partially undressed in my room made him ill. When he finished, Jackson came over to the side of my bed, bent down, and kissed my forehead. "I'll come back if you need me. Call, text, instant message me, or send up a smoke signal," he joked.

"I will. Thank you," I said.

He then turned around and looked down at Marcus. Jackson towered a full foot above him, and Marcus had to looked up to meet his gaze. "I look forward to that discussion."

"No doubt," said Marcus. "Real soon—you know you're in violation of a code that a so-called *friend* should never break."

"Fuck you and your man code. You don't deserve her. See you later, Natalie."

Marcus maintained his composure. "Jackson, you need to be real easy and choose your next words carefully."

"Whenever you ready, playboy," said Jackson and walked out of the room.

Neither Marcus nor I said a word until we heard the front door shut. I studied him. I missed him.

The first thing he said was, "What's going on with you two?"

"You're in no position to ask me what I do with other people. You recently slept with your ex-girlfriend and you dated and knocked up one of her closest friends. I suggest you put away all judgment because you have been *in violation*, as you say, for quite some time."

Marcus took a deep breath and ran his hand through his hair. The action couldn't have made it any worse than it already was. It hadn't been cut, combed, or brushed, and there were small flecks of lint in it. It also appeared wet, as if he had just taken a shower. I'd never known him to go without a haircut for more than a week.

I sat up a little more in my bed and listened to the rain beating against the window as I continued to examine him. I could tell the silence was making him uncomfortable. I liked that. I was in no hurry to continue talking. After a few seconds I said, "Now, what's going on with you? You look like hell."

Marcus came over and adjusted the pillows behind me to help make me more comfortable. "Long story. It's a combination of things," he said. "I will be honest and say that I haven't been on my 'A' game lately, but *these* clothes were a last-minute kind of deal helping someone out. We can talk about that later."

"Don't tell me that Marcus Colbert has a conscience. Could he really be capable of caring for someone other than himself?"

He moved closer and pulled my covers back to expose my midsection. My nightgown was still gathered around my waist where Jackson left it earlier. I now had on panties though.

"What are you doing?"

"I care about this little guy," he said and pushed my gown up further to reveal my full belly. It was stretched completely out of proportion and massive. I felt so unattractive, but I must not have looked too bad if Jackson wanted to bed me. He began rubbing his hands over my stomach in a slow circular motion. "I've missed him." He paused and looked at me. "And his mother."

I didn't say anything. I just closed my eyes and enjoyed the feel of his hands on my flesh. They were soft and soothing. They felt safe, warm, and familiar. They felt like home. Trenton moved in response. I'm sure he missed him too. Then I felt our son press something against the inside of my abdomen. I opened my eyes and looked down. To both our surprise, you could clearly see the imprint of a tiny hand on the outside. Four little fingers and a thumb as if he was reaching out to touch his daddy. I winched a little from the pressure. Marcus bent down and kissed his handprint, and then placed his larger one on top of it. "Hey, little man. I got you. Don't you ever worry. Daddy's back," he said.

It was a touching moment, but it was hard for me to enjoy it. I hadn't seen him in 2 weeks, but I had a good idea where he might have been spending his time. He then looked up at me and smiled. Normally, that smile would make me melt like butter, but now, in this moment, it only made me upset. How dare he come in my house without my permission as if he belonged here! I had to admit, though, that I was happy to have an excuse to ask Jackson to leave. After experiencing his mediocre cunnilingus technique, I wasn't exactly feeling the warm fuzzies toward him. I was actually surer than ever that we wouldn't be more than just friends.

"Those things are getting huge," Marcus said eyeing my breasts through my nightgown. He reached up to grab one, and I slapped his hand.

"Ouch!"

"How's Chanel?" I asked.

Chapter 16

Marcus

As I sat in the room that was once a place that was reserved solely for pleasure principals, I realized that it was now the residence of broken hearts and scarred egos. I made sure to check mine at the door before I arrived at Natalie's place. However, I was caught off guard by not the presence of another man, but *whom* that man was. Jackson and I never had that *talk* I intended to have with him after the last time I witnessed how close he and Natalie had become. The only part that made me hesitant was the fact that it was indeed my actions acting as the magnet that pulled them together.

I immediately thought about what that old man had said, "I can't allow another man to do *my* job." But what was *my* job? My job as a father-to-be was inevitable, but what was my job with Natalie?

Natalie and I sat in silence as we both attempted to read through the windows of each other's soul. Jackson was in the rearview of my concerns. He wasn't my competition. And it was confirmed that he was not my friend. He was an opportunist—always had been since I'd known him. He really didn't matter to me after I saw the imprint of my son's hand. It was as if he were reaching out to me to remind me that he was there and he needed me.

I noticed how Natalie was looking over my new rugged facial hair. Her eyes scoured me down from head to toe. I attempted to break the awkwardness by mentioning the swelling of her breasts. I could tell that she wanted to open up, but that hard exterior returned as she asked me about Chanel. There was no reason to lie. All the cards were faceup on the table anyway.

I ran my hands over the soft coils of hair on my head as I replied, "We talked."

"You talked? *And*?"

"We discussed the situation at hand—*ours* too."

"*Ours*?"

Her short, one-word replies held the same weight as a full sentence. "We had a very detailed conversation. We laid all of our faults on the table. I apologized for my actions. Honestly, she was an innocent bystander in the middle of my madness." I stood up and began to pace the room. "Honestly, I'm tired of apologizing too." Her eyebrows coiled up which indicated she didn't like my last statement. "All I'm saying is—I'm tired of being in positions to have to apologize."

She nodded. "I can understand that, Marcus." Her eyes found empty space in the room. "So, where does that leave y'all—you and Chanel?"

"We understand that we made adult decisions, so we must now handle them as such."

"What does that mean?"

"That means I've had to make some tough decisions."

"What did you decide?"

As she asked that question, our eyes locked. I saw the seriousness etched upon her face meshing with the pain of her tone. "That's why I'm here, Natalie." I gracefully brushed aside the strands of hair that had escaped her ponytail and were on her face. As my hand grazed her skin lightly, I continued with a whisper, "I'm here."

She studied my face . . . confused between the love she still had in her heart and the doubt she had in her mind.

Now holding her hand, I said, "Listen, we're not going to have all the answers tonight or tomorrow. *However*, we have to trust the process. A fresh start for us would be to become friends. I don't think we ever had the chance to allow our friendship to grow."

She remained silent. I felt her squeeze my hand slightly. It was as if her heart was overtaking her mind. They say love conquers all. It acts as a sealant to the mind, body, and soul.

She sighed, looked across at me, and sighed again.

She then said, "About Jackson—"

Chapter 17

Natalie

"Jackson has asked me to give us a try. He's completely willing to date me while I carry, give birth, *and* raise your child. I'll be honest. It's tempting. I've worked with him for years, and he's a pretty good guy. He's never caused me pain the way you have, and somehow, I don't think he would. But there's one problem."

Marcus looked at me with empty eyes. It was evident he didn't like the notion of Jackson being my man. "What's that?" he asked.

"I'm not all that attracted to him, *and* I'm in love with my child's father. It's easy for you to say let's be friends, but I'm way past that stage, Marcus. I don't have a problem with getting to know each other better on a different level, but if you're asking me to act like I don't wake up every morning wanting to cover that face in kisses and wishing that *I* was wearing your ring in addition to carrying your child—I can't. Even though your actions have ripped into my heart, I still love you. But the problem I have with you is trust. I don't trust you, Marcus Colbert. You've got a cold heart. Only a man with a cold heart could repeatedly cause the pain you've caused me. For God's sake, I'm carrying *your* baby. For that alone I deserve some respect."

Marcus looked at me and for the first time, I saw regret. "Natalie, I was wrong. Dead wrong and I'm sorry. I'll never be perfect, but believe me when I say I've seen the error of my ways and going forward, I will take into account how my actions will impact you and Trenton."

"But what about Chanel? You have no idea how much it hurts knowing that you'll be leaving me and our son to go check on her and the child she has growing inside of her. You'll be attending doctor's appointments and a baby shower. I've been so screwed up I haven't even had a baby shower. I just wasn't in the mood to pretend like I'm happy. What pregnant woman doesn't even a have a baby shower, Marcus?"

"Then, let's have a baby shower," he said.

"Whaaat? Don't be ridiculous. I'm due any day now. Besides, I've already purchased most of the stuff the baby will need online. It's over there in the corner." I pointed toward the boxes. Marcus turned around and eyeballed them briefly.

"Jackson agreed to come help me put the nursery together. I only have one bedroom, so Trenton will have to be in here with me," I continued.

"Natalie, I thought we agreed that you and the baby would stay with me after the birth. I have plenty of space. I already cleaned out one of the extra rooms for a nursery."

"That was before you slept with Lisa and before I found out about Chanel. We belong here. This is *our* home. No one is going to make me cry, break my heart, or have another little bastard running around for my baby to have to compete with for affection here."

I could tell my words hurt Marcus, but I didn't care. Technically, my baby was a bastard too, but he got my point. My baby and I needed to be protected from the selfishness of his father. At least until I was sure Marcus meant what he said about not doing anything that he would need to apologize for later.

"Okay. I won't argue with you. I probably deserve that, but Jackson will not be putting together my child's crib. I'll take care of it, and I'm still throwing you a baby shower. You don't have to lift a finger. All you'll have to do is comb your hair and not wear gowns where everyone can see those big pretty nipples of yours."

He licked his lips, then reached in his pocket and pulled out his cell phone and hit a button to dial a preprogrammed number. Whoever it was picked up on the second ring. Before they could say a word, Marcus said, "Ma, I'm at Chanel's. I need your help. We're throwing her a baby shower . . ." Marcus realized what he had done and stopped talking. He then hit himself in the forehead with the palm of his hand and said, "Shit!"

I rolled my eyes. Marcus didn't know what he wanted or who he wanted. He was so confused that he'd just called me Chanel.

"Get out!" I screamed.

"I'm sorry, Natalie. You know I meant you." I heard Mrs. Colbert screaming in the background, but I had no idea what she was saying. "Ma, I'll call you back," said Marcus and hung up.

He should be glad that I'm bedridden or I probably would have gone to the kitchen to get a knife and stabbed him. "Get out! I don't want to be your friend, Marcus. Being with you equals pain and disappointment. Nothing but pain and disappointment!" I pulled the pillows from behind me and hurled one at him. It landed in his chest and hit the floor. I threw that other one, and he caught it. I looked at him and burst into tears. "It hurts, Marcus. No matter what I do, I'm never foremost in your thoughts. It's not fair because you're all I want. Jackson ate me out today, and you know what I was thinking about the entire time? You!! How I wished it was *you*! How good you make me feel when I'm with *you*!"

Marcus's eyes became so big I thought they were going to pop out of his head. "You let Jackson eat you out and you're sitting up here trying to make me feel guilty? Telling me you love *me* and you allowed *that*?" He paused and ran a hand through his hair. I didn't mean to tell him that, but maybe Marcus deserved some of his own medicine. Maybe I should start operating with no regard for what he thinks or feels. He took a deep breath and smiled. "You know what? I think you're right, Natalie. Every time I'm around you. I make you cry. I'm sorry, but I'm going to make it up to you. I'm not leaving. You can't push me away anymore. I won't let you. You gotta believe me when I say I'm going to get my shit together, and from the sound of it—*you* should do the same. I'll be in the living room planning a baby shower. Get some rest and from now on, Jackson is no longer allowed anywhere near you. I'll take care of that too."

He walked out, and my phone rang. It was Mrs. Colbert. Right now, I could use a mother even if it wasn't mine. I wiped the tears streaming down my face and said, "Hello."

"My son is an idiot," she said.

"I know," I sobbed.

"But he is right. You do need a baby shower. I didn't bring it up before because I knew you weren't really feeling up to it, but this is your first child and my first grandchild. Would you do me the honor of letting Marcus and me throw you a baby shower?"

"Mrs. Colbert, I appreciate the sentiment but—"

"Natalie, babies are expensive. I'm sure you and Marcus could use help purchasing all those baby bottles, wipes, Pampers, and such. Be practical, child. And remember, you aren't working right now and don't have a job to go back to."

I had to admit she had a point. I let out a large sigh and said, "Okay, but just a few people."

"Fantastic. It will be soon since I know the baby is due any day now. How's the day after tomorrow?"

"I can't think of anyplace I have to be," I joked.

"Great. Marcus will work on the guest list and his sister and I will handle everything else. Thank you for making an old woman's day. I love you, Natalie. And there's nothing you can do about it. Please forgive my son, the idiot's slip of the tongue."

"I'll think about it. I love you too, Mrs. Colbert," I said before we said our good-byes. I had grown quite attached to her over the past few months. The more Marcus messed up, the nicer she was to me, as if she was trying to compensate for her son's shortcomings.

Marcus walked back in with a large bowl and a face-cloth and a towel. He was taking careful steps like he was trying not to spill its contents. I rolled my eyes at him. "What are you doing?"

"I'm going to clean you up. I don't know where that backstabber's mouth has been. I gotta get you cleaned up before you develop the yeast infection from hell and my son ends up with some nasty rash while inside the womb."

I laughed. "Boy, you are crazy!"

"Look, Natalie, I'm not perfect, and I've been wrong, but I plan to do better. All I ask is you give me a chance."

I nodded to signify I would.

"Yep. Now take that gown off—doctor's order. I'm about to give you the most sensual sponge bath you've ever had. You can stay angry at me all you want, little lady, but that's not gonna deter me from doing what I need and want to do. So let the pleasure begin on behalf of . . . The Marcus Colbert Experience."

I could have stayed mad at him, but it really served no purpose. We had to stop this vicious cycle we were on. My son needed his father, and truth be told, I needed him too. We would have to raise this child together, and it would go smoother if we were on good terms. I closed my eyes and relaxed as Marcus proceeded to deliver on his promise. It was definitely the most memorable sponge bath I had ever had. I couldn't figure out what was soaking the sheets more, me or the warm soapy water he was using to bathe me. Afterward, he massaged almost every inch of me. I was extremely relaxed. My mind felt at ease and so did my body. I looked forward to Trenton vacating the premises so we could make love again.

Afterward, he changed the sheets, and then crawled in the bed next to me. I felt good. I felt satisfied, and I felt wanted, but I didn't feel loved. There was one burning question in my mind that I had to ask, and I hoped that it wouldn't ruin our moment.

"Marcus, why are you choosing me? You have an opportunity to have the connection you say we don't have with Chanel and a baby along with it. I gave you an out, and I promised that I wouldn't interfere. Why are you here asking me to give *us* another try?"

Marcus laughed. "Woman, you always want to talk at the most interesting times." He kissed me on my neck and nuzzled his nose in it. "I love you, Natalie. It's just a different kind of love than what I'm used to, and you love me in a way no one else has. Also, there's no baggage with us. I don't have to compete with your career. I don't have any guilt for tearing up a friendship or guilt for knowing that the only reason I chose Chanel is because she was the next best thing to Lisa. I won't lie, a lot of my actions were a result of me trying to get over Lisa in a very unhealthy way. But I'm done with that. I'm moving on, and I chose you because you're you. You and I are actually quite easy, but my bad judgment has been complicating things. I would be doing myself, you, and our son a disservice if I didn't see this thing through. We have some work to do, but I think in the end, it will be worth it."

I wasn't quite sure how I felt about his answer. I knew he wasn't over Lisa yet, but at least he was no longer denying it. It was nice to be seen as a priority, but I wondered how long that would last.

Marcus's phone chimed indicating that he got a text message. He got it off the nightstand and did something he had never done before. He checked it in my line of sight.

"No more secrets," he said. I scanned it quickly. It was from Lisa.

YOU FUCKING BASTARD!! IT'S BAD ENOUGH YOU DATE ONE OF MY FRIENDS BUT YOU GET HER PREGNANT TOO. YOU ARE AN ASSHOLE OF EPIC PROPORTIONS.

DELETE MY NUMBER AND NEVER CONTACT ME AGAIN! I REGRET THE DAY I MET YOU. YOU ARE SELFISH AS HELL.

"What are you going to do?" I said.

"Honor her wishes. I've caused her, you, and Chanel enough pain." He then went to his contacts and deleted her number. "I have more important things to worry about. I'm here, Natalie, and I'm not going anywhere." Then he nuzzled my neck again.

"That's really good to hear, Marcus. One more thing. Your sister has been hanging out in Murfreesboro a lot. Does she have a good friend there? I've been checking my car's GPS occasionally, and I just thought that was quite a distance for a teenager to be going on the regular. Not to mention the miles she's putting on my car," I said.

"Murfreesboro? It's not that far but she has no business there. Not that I know of. I'll ask my mom about it tomorrow," he said before draping an arm over me. Then we both drifted to sleep. I really missed this man.

Chapter 18

Marcus

I woke up fresh, renewed, and rejuvenated. The beam of light that snuck its way underneath the blinds from Natalie's window was my awakening. Natalie was still sleep. I stared at her momentarily. The innocence of a sleeping face is something I've always been a sucker for. I guess it's the fact that sleep is a period where your mind is at ease—peaceful. Her head was resting atop my arm. The wind from every one of her breaths found its way to my neck. She looked good to my eyes. She was glowing. It was as if I was viewing her for the first time. Not only was I mentally fresh, renewed, and rejuvenated, but my heart was as well.

I was able to wedge myself from under Natalie without interrupting her peacefulness. I wondered how many sleepless nights she'd had on my behalf. I gently stroked her face before I proceeded to kiss her on the forehead. I looked down at her protruding stomach and gently rubbed her there as well.

As I sat on the edge of the bed, I bowed my head and said a prayer to myself. I then looked over the room and made some mental notes. As I stood to my feet, I grabbed the clothes hamper that was in front of her bathroom door. I noticed there were a couple of piles of unwashed clothing hiding behind the bathroom door. Without a second thought, I gathered them all, including the ones in the hamper, and headed to the washer.

I began to laugh at myself a little. My childhood flashed across my mind. I'd always hated cleaning up on Saturday mornings with my mother. Now, days such as this were therapy for me. As I closed the door to the washing machine, I proceeded to fold the leftover clothes from the dryer and once I was finished I properly placed them in her dresser. I was maneuvering like a thief in the night being careful as to not wake her up.

As I walked out of her bedroom, I closed the door, slowly making my way to the kitchen. With all the cleaning utensils at my disposal, I went to work: dishes, dusting, moping, and sweeping. You would have thought I was a teenager covering up a hellacious house party from my parents. I put on a pot of coffee before I sat down to catch up on the latest book I was reading on my phone. No sooner than I sat down, I heard the door open. I looked over my shoulder thinking it was Natalie awaking from her peace. At that moment, my fresh, renewed, and rejuvenated spirit went back to a dark place.

Standing in the middle of the kitchen was Jackson holding a bag of bagels and coffee in hand. He placed them on the table and slowly placed the key back in his pocket. He wanted to be sure that I knew that *he* had the key. Key to *what* would be the question of the day. Yes, he may have had the key to the door, but I had *the key* to Natalie's *heart.* His eyes were almost as dark as the tailored suit that covered his body. He pulled out a chair and permitted himself to take a seat. The smell of a cigar he must have recently smoked began to hover. Trying to hold my anger within, I braced myself.

"What are you doing here, Jackson? I thought I made myself perfectly clear in the text I sent last night—I don't—*we* don't want you around."

A slight smirk graced his mischievous face. "Marcus, are we really gonna do this?"

Perplexed by the question, I asked, "Do what?"

In an attempt to affirm or intimidate, Jackson stared me straight in my eyes as he replied, "Sit up here and pretend that you actually give a fuck about Natalie."

I could tell that he was playing chess within his mind. I studied his eyes as I replied, "Why is that of any concern to you?"

"Come on, Marcus, enough of the bullshit. You and I both know that this is going to end one of two ways."

"And what ways are those?"

Jackson leaned back, crossed his leg, and folded his arms. "You mess up and she comes running back to me, or she comes to her senses and realized I'm the best choice. So, let's just expedite this process by you walking away and leaving me with what is mine."

"Yours?"

He leaned in closer. "Yes. Mine."

I stood up staring down at Jackson as this was the only way I would ever tower over him physically. My cool, calm, and collected demeanor was bending, but I refused to let it break. "You know what, Jackson? This doesn't even surprise me."

Now standing up to match my stance and towering over me, Jackson replied, "What doesn't?"

"Ever since we've known each other, I've always had the sense that you were *jealous* of me."

Jackson began to laugh my response off. "Jealous?" With an annoying smirk on his face he continued,

"Marcus, please tell me what in the hell I have to be jealous of you about? What is it that *you* have that *I* don't have—times three?"

"That's the point, Jackson. You can have everything in the world, but deep down inside, you're still never satisfied until you have the plus one over *me*." I could tell I had struck a nerve. "Over *me*, Jackson—you're supposed to be a brother. When I first got the condo, you moved into a half-million-dollar house. When I got the whip, you popped up with the expensive truck when you already had a nice car even though it was a couple of years older than mine. Oh yeah, I know about that shit you tried to pull with Lisa too."

His eyes looked of defeat, which could be dangerous. When a man has recognized that he has been figured out or defeated, anger could be the replacement—dangerous anger.

I continued. "But there is one thing you could never do, Jackson."

He searched my eyes for the answer.

"Be me—even Ashley knew that."

Checkmate. That was the move I'd been calculating this entire time. I've always had my intuitions about Jackson. My father always told me to keep friends close, but enemies closer. However, over time, I'd learned to overlook Jackson's flaws in terms of friendship and brotherhood. This wasn't the first time Jackson wanted something or *someone* that he couldn't have on the account of me. Until recently, I thought he was over competing with me.

Back in grad school, Jackson had fallen hard for a gorgeous young lady by the name of Ashley. I was dating Lisa at the time but we weren't serious yet. So Jackson was looking for his "plus-one." After numerous failed attempts at getting Ashley to commit to a date, she finally just told him the truth. She told him that she was interested in me, not him. He was stupefied because he had the nice car, fancy apartment, and job. I didn't have much of anything at that point in my life. I was a struggling student. He couldn't understand why she would pick *me* over him. That's when all the snide remarks and hidden jealousy began. The fact that he wanted someone that wanted me, but I didn't want in return bothered him to the core. So much so that he would drop slick little innuendos to Lisa about me. He went so far as to attempt to kiss her on one occasion in my absence. He blamed it on the liquor as he was rejected. I never brought it up as a promise to Lisa, but from that point on, Jackson became the enemy that I kept close.

Jackson looked down at the table, and then back up at me. Before I knew it, he had made a swing toward my face. Thank God for quick reflexes, because that blow could have been damaging. The force was so hard, it made his body lunge forward, straight into the kitchen counter. The impact made a couple of glasses shatter to the floor. Now embarrassed and even more agitated, he turned with even more fury in his eyes. Walking toward me, you could hear the glass mashing and cracking underneath his dress shoes. With protruding veins sticking out from his neck he said, "You want some honesty? Truth be told, I've never liked your ass."

My hands grasped the arm of the chair that was to my left. As I proceeded to pick it up and draw back, I heard someone scream my name. I looked back and saw Natalie with tears in her eyes.

"Stop it. Both of you—just stop it," she yelled. "I'm sick of it all. Marcus, please leave."

"But—"

"Go, Marcus, please."

With a smirk on his face, Jackson replied, "Yeah, leave, you son of a bitch." He pushed aside some glass with his foot and walked toward Natalie. He placed his hand over her stomach and said, "Baby, I knew you would come back to me. We can do this—*together*—me, you, and this baby."

As I was making my way to the door I looked back and saw a smile flash over Natalie's face. It was immediately replaced with a scowl like I'd never seen. She looked at Jackson with eyes of fire and said, "You listen, and you listen good, Jackson. I heard everything. It's obvious that you've been using my times of pain and strife as your personal little playground. You don't want or care for me. You're just in love with the idea of being with me to spite Marcus. I want you to leave."

Clutching his suit jacket, Jackson pleaded, "Baby, listen. Baby, please—"

"LEAVE, Jackson," she said a little more forcefully.

"Baby, just listen. Hear me out."

"Jackson, I swear before God himself, if I have to tell you to leave one more time, I may do something we'll both regret."

Jackson saw that her eyes had been fixated on a sharp piece of glass that was near her foot.

That smirk returned, and he took his jacket off his shoulder and held it with his index finger. "So this is how you gonna do *me*? After *all* I've done for your ungrateful ass? Who do you think got you that bonus? Me. Who do you think paid for most of that shit in that room for that baby? Me. Who stayed up with your crazy ass all those long hours? Who else is going to treat a basic girl like you, like a queen, which is much more than what *you* are?"

I could no longer just stand there and allow him to keep insulting the mother of my child. I grabbed him by the collar and pulled him toward the door. We tussled all the way through the living room, neither getting the better of the other. I finally got some leverage and was able to drag him outside.

I'll admit, mixed in with my anger was hurt as well. Even though I'd always known who Jackson really was, he still had some type of impact and influence over my life as I entered manhood. He was a couple of years ahead of me, so in essence, he was indeed like a big brother.

With his collar in my hands, both of us huffing and puffing, the smoking getting the best of Jackson, I said, "I want you to leave, Jackson, and never come back around here," with short spurts of breaks in between each couple of words. At that point, I struck him in his face to express my seriousness. I hit him again to make my point clearer. He attempted to escape from my grasp, but before I let him go, I went in his pocket and took what was mine.

"*Now* you can leave," I said as I held the key in my hand.

He pulled back, fixed his tie, and rubbed a little of the blood from his nose that was beginning to leak. Without saying a word, he turned and walked away. I stared him down until I saw his truck leave the premises.

Looking at the key in my hand, I looked over my shoulder and saw Natalie standing in the apartment doorway with her hand on her belly.

"Here's your key. I'll leave now, Natalie."

"Where are you going?" she asked in a low tone.

"You asked me to leave—remember?"

"I meant the room, not the apartment."

"So, you're not mad at me? You want me to stay?"

She didn't answer me. She closed the space between us and passionately kissed my lips. Then she brushed her hand across my lip. "You're bleeding."

"Love is war at times," I replied.

Her eyes searched mine. "Love?"

I nodded and smiled.

"Come on in here so I can clean you up. We'll talk about this love thing later."

I smiled and followed her lead.

Chapter 19

Natalie

I must admit having a man defend my honor was kind of cool. I felt like that mythological chick, Helen of Troy. An entire war started because two men wanted her. I was glad Marcus kicked Jackson's butt. He deserved an Oscar for his performance of a man who loved me and truly wanted what was best for me. The whole time he just wanted to hurt Marcus. Marcus and I walked into my apartment arm in arm as he escorted me back to my bed.

"I'll clean myself up," he said. "You're not supposed to be out of bed. What were you thinking? You could have gone into labor."

Marcus was so cute when he chastised me. It felt good knowing that he genuinely cared. "I was thinking that I didn't want bloodshed in my home. The moment I heard Jackson's voice, I knew there was going to be trouble."

"You must have supersonic hearing or something. I thought you were asleep."

"I was, but Grammy called to tell me that her gout flared up again and she wouldn't be able to get back to Nashville as quickly as she thought."

He made an exaggerated sad face and said, "I'm *so* disappointed."

"Shut up, boy! You know you don't like my Grammy"

He flashed me that smile I love so much. "She's okay . . . if you like overbearing old ladies with foul mouths."

He then raised an eyebrow and said, "So you gave Jackson a key?"

I laughed. "That's what's on your mind right now? No, I did not. A few weeks ago he went to the store for me and I gave him my keys so he could get back in without me having to get out of the bed. While he was out, he took the liberty of making himself a key."

"That sounds like him," muttered Marcus. "Did he really buy the stuff for the baby?"

"I guess. When he saw me making the orders he handed me his credit card and told me to put them on there."

Marcus ran his hand through his hair. Then, licked the corner of his bruised lip. "Do you know how much he spent?"

I sat down on my bed. "What is this? Twenty-One Questions? Yes, I have the receipts in my e-mail."

"It's as many questions that I need to get the answers I want," he said before gently tickling my sides. I was too big to escape him so my only option was to squirm and giggle until he stopped. He laughed too because he enjoyed seeing me squirm. After we both regained our composure, he said, "I want you to calculate the total, and then tell me how much it is so I can give him back his money. I don't want that bastard providing for our child."

Pride can be such a stupid thing. I personally could care less if Jackson bought our child's necessities. That's more money we have to spend on other things, but I knew better than to argue with Marcus about this one. So, I just nodded my head in agreement. What difference did it make? It wasn't my money either way.

"Okay. Consider it done," I said. I actually had a request of my own. "Marcus, after the baby is born, I want to go back to school and finish getting my degree. I'm going to really need you to step up and support me when I do."

"Natalie, I have no problem with that, but where is this coming from?"

"When I first got pregnant, you told me that there wasn't much depth to me. I seemed 'shallow,' and then Jackson just called me basic. If you two see me that way, and you know me, I wonder what the rest of the world thinks. They probably see me as just some semi-intelligent woman who can't do better than being a secretary too. People probably think I got pregnant by you on purpose so you can 'upgrade' me."

Marcus kissed my cheek. "Baby, I never should have said that. I was wrong. I said that before I got to know you and learned how wonderful and talented you are. You make money trading stock options. I have no idea how to do that. You were studying to get your producer's license which you can still do with another company. I bet you get a job offer in no time once you put your résumé back out there." He ran his hand over the top of my head. "Do you want me to kick Jackson's ass again? I will if it will make you feel better."

I touched his bruised face. "Thanks, slugger, but I think there's been enough rough housing for today. And thanks for the vote of confidence, but I'm going back to school. It's not just for me, but for Trenton too. I want him to be proud of both his parents. Wouldn't you like to be able to brag on the mother of your child? I think 'Dr. Natalie Tellis' has a nice ring to it, don't you?"

"Yeah, but I like 'Dr. Natalie T. Colbert' better," he said.

I had to admit that it did sound nice, but it was too early for me to be getting my hopes up. Marcus and I still had a lot of work to do on our relationship. I was determined not to get hurt again. It was also too soon for me to talk about letting my guard completely down.

"I'm going to make you prouder than you've ever been. Prouder than you were of Lisa and Chanel put together," I said.

Marcus stopped and looked at me. "Whoa. Wait a minute. I don't want you comparing yourself to them. They're in my rear view. You and Trenton are what's in front of me. I *am* proud of you, Natalie. The way you've been holding it down without me. Even though I hurt you, you've still been doing what you have to do. You're an amazing woman, and you're going to be an amazing mother." He kissed me on the forehead before gently guiding me beneath the down-filled duvet on my bed. "Now, let me get cleaned up so I can go baby shower shopping. Oh, I forgot to tell you that my mother and I changed the date."

"Really. What did she change it to?"

"Today."

I bolted straight up. "What? Today? I'm a mess. My hair needs to be washed, and I don't have anything to wear."

"Relax. I've got everything covered. My mother and I decided the sooner the better since you're due any day now. In roughly 9 hours, you will be the center of attention at your own baby shower. Now, smile. This is a good thing."

I let out a sigh and looked around my room. I still had several items that needed to be picked up, and although Marcus had started cleaning, he didn't finish. I really wished they had run this by me first. I had nothing to smile about. I was about to voice my displeasure when the doorbell rang.

"Who is that?" I asked.

Marcus smiled like he had been keeping secret. "It's probably my sister. I told her to come sit with you and help you get ready. It will also give you a chance to get her to tell you why she is spending so much time in Murfreesboro."

"Marcus, don't put me in the middle of this!"

"I'm not, but she won't talk to my mother, and she's worried. She's become disrespectful, defiant, and she keeps staying out later and later. She told my mother she was at cheerleading practice, but we found out last week she quit the squad. When my mom asks where she's been, she just lies. You two have a special relationship, and I know she'll tell you what's going on before she'd ever tell her big brother. Besides, she has been driving your car to do Lord knows what. Wouldn't you like to know what it is?"

I had to admit he was right. If she was taking my car someplace where it could get stripped or carjacked, I needed to know. Marcus walked out of the room to let her in. Two seconds later, Mia bounced in with a huge grin on her face. I guess it was her face. She had on so much makeup I barely even recognized her. When I met this woman-child, she barely wore lip gloss, and now she was in full makeup with expertly arched eyebrows and nose contouring. It was pretty, but it made her look at least 10 years older than her 17-year-old self. It was a bit much for my taste. Mia would be graduating from high school soon and was expected to go to Tennessee State University on a cheerleading scholarship in the fall, although she didn't need it. The girl was so smart she'd gotten over $50,000 worth of independent scholarships. The top she wore had a plunging neckline exposing the tops of her small breasts, and her pants were so tight I wondered if they were cutting off her circulation. It was obvious she was trying to impress someone, but who and why were the questions I needed answers to.

She came over and gave me a tight hug. "Hey, Natalie. How are you? Sorry it took me so long to come see you, but you know how senior year can be . . . busy, busy busy . . . school, cheerleading, senior activities, and getting the money to pay for them. I'm working a lot of hours at the new job I got."

I hugged her back. The girl had on so much perfume I started to cough. It would have been a nice fragrance if it wasn't so potent. "Yeah. I'm sure. Where are you working?" I asked in between coughs.

"Oh, this little pizza place in the mall," she answered.

I knew she was doing more than working. Marcus walked back in the room and headed to the bathroom to take a shower.

"Don't mind me, ladies," he said before he closed the door.

Once I was sure he couldn't hear us I said, "You're having sex, aren't you?"

The question caught her completely off guard.

"No. I mean yes. I mean no. Maybe a little."

"Either you are or you aren't. And he's older, isn't he?"

In a matter of seconds, sweat began to bead on her forehead and her eyes roamed across the room. She and I had a good relationship. We actually used to talk quite a bit before she gained use of my car and was gone all the time. She trusted me, but she also knew not to lie to me. "Not much older. He goes the Middle Tennessee State University, and he's only a junior."

"A junior?! That makes him at least 20. Girl, have you lost your mind? That's a grown man, and technically, you're still a child. That's illegal. It's called statutory rape, and do you know what your parents or Marcus will do if they find out?"

We heard the water stop, and then the door opened, but the only thing to exit the bathroom was steam. We then heard Marcus brushing his teeth.

Mia lowered her voice to almost a whisper. "It's not that serious, and I'll be 18 in a couple of months. I'm going to tell them, but I want to wait until we're both of legal age. Please don't snitch on me."

This girl was being turned out, and she expected me to keep quiet. Lord, give me strength! We heard Marcus rinse his mouth and spit before he walked out of the bathroom with a towel on. We both froze. He eyed us both suspiciously, but didn't say a word as he grabbed his clothes off the chaise and headed back in the bathroom.

Mia came close to me and sat herself and her oversized Michael Kors purse Marcus got her for Christmas. "Sebastian is a really nice guy. He's on the Dean's List. He's the president of the Black Student Association, and we're not even serious. We're just kicking it."

I abhor that phrase with a passion. Some man who was trying to avoid commitment came up with that term to help him explain to women why it was all right for them to constantly sleep together with no clear definition of where they're headed.

I gave a nervous laugh. "You are too young to be 'kicking it.' What do you know about it anyway?"

She laid her head on my shoulder like a child. "Please calm down, Natalie, because if you go into labor, everyone will blame me. I know a lot. I know that's how you got pregnant. You and my brother weren't even dating, and voilà! I've got a nephew on the way."

"Exactly," I said. "Why would you want to put yourself in the position I'm in? You know what your brother has put me through."

"That's because you let your heart get involved. I won't let that happen, and I won't get pregnant. I'm on birth control, and I use condoms with him and whoever else I'm sleeping with."

My body jolted, causing her to remove her head from my shoulder. "There's more than one?!"

Mia looked at me and nodded her head. I searched her eyes looking for a shred of common sense. She was raised in the same Christian household as Marcus. What happened to these two? Were they not listening? Did they block out all those years of Sunday morning services, Bible study, and vacation Bible school?

She answered. "Yeah. I'm not in a relationship, so I can sleep with whoever I want. If guys can sleep with multiple women, why can't we? I get so tired of that double standard bullshit. It's a new day. No man owns me. I fuck who I want. It's no big deal. It's just sex. And they all fine too. You should see the body on Samson, and he has a *huge* thang. I thought I wouldn't be able to handle it, but I took it like a pro."

Like a pro ho, I thought. My head started to hurt. My boyfriend's little sister was sitting on my bed telling me she was hot in the pants, and *we* were to thank for setting the example. Why wasn't she paying attention to her parents instead of us? They were the ones with the great relationship. Marcus and I were dysfunctional at best. We had to fix this, but I'd have to figure out how later.

Just then, Marcus came out of the bathroom looking like a million bucks. His khakis and shirt he wore were a little wrinkled, but they fit him in all the right places. I loved the way his shirts clung to his upper body showing off his chest and arms. Any other time I would have stopped what I was doing and stared in awe, but right now, I was ashamed of him and us. Not because he'd done anything wrong, but because I realized how our actions have affected not only the child growing inside me, but the child right in front of us who has been observing our actions and taking it all in. We haven't been setting a good example of what a healthy, loving relationship looks like.

He grabbed his keys off the chaise and said, "Okay. I'm off to get a haircut and all the goodies for tonight. Mia, make sure she looks nice. Curl her hair or something. We can retire that ponytail for a day or two." He came over and kissed me on the lips. He then searched my eyes for some indication that everything was okay.

I smiled and squeezed his hand to indicate that it was, even though it wasn't.

"I'll be back in a couple of hours," he said and with that, he disappeared from my room.

The little idiot in front of me continued to try to plead her case. "We're *not* serious so we both agreed it was all right to sleep with other people. All his friends do it. They have these parties where you come with one person and leave with another."

I grabbed my chest as if I were clutching a strand of pearls. "He's a swinger, and you, young lady, are too young to be swinging! I did not let you borrow my car so you can have a sexual awakening with college men."

"Technically, I'm in college too. I've been accepted. I just haven't started my classes. Stop being so old-fashioned. Of all the people who would understand me having my needs taken care of, I thought it would be you. My hormones are raging, and I got tired of masturbating."

"Why did you quit the cheerleading squad?"

"You know? Well, Sebastian is an intellectual, and he said cheerleading is misogynistic and demoralizing for women because it causes us to use our looks and our bodies to gain attention rather than our minds. I'm a straight-A student and there's no reason for me to be shaking my pom-poms when I could be giving lectures and mentoring youth with that time."

"What the hell, Mia? What do you think you're using when you're fucking this guy and his friends . . . *your* body, that's what. He's manipulating your young mind and emotions to separate you from the things you love and mold you into what he wants you to be. You and I both know you're not giving lectures while he uses you as his human pocket pussy. Before he peels your clothes off, they're sizing you up like meat on a platter. And guess what? After they have all had a turn, they discuss what they did and what you did like some common whore walking down the street. That intellectual BS was just a ploy to lure in an impressionable girl like you. You should never give up something you really enjoy for a man who's not even yours. You and Marcus both grew up in a loving household with two faithful parents, and I swear, both of you act like monogamy and commitment are foreign topics."

"I have no desire to be like my mother. Her entire life revolves around my father and her kids. She has nothing for herself. From dusk 'til dawn she caters to the needs of others. Whoever I'm with is going to understand that I have a career and hobbies too. I knew you wouldn't understand. Let's change the subject. I'm almost grown, and I don't need you or anybody else's permission to live my life."

"You may be almost an adult in age, but that mind of yours has a lot of maturing to do." The room suddenly grew warm, and now I was the one sweating. I couldn't believe what I was hearing. I took a swig of the container full of water I generally keep near my bed. It hadn't been changed since yesterday so the water was room temperature. The liquid quenched my thirst, but it was far from refreshing.

Mia waved her hand in the air as if she was trying to dismiss the subject. "It's not that big of a deal. At my age, it's normal to have sex. Let's try to find you something to wear."

I honestly didn't know what to say or do at that moment, so I welcomed the change of subject. We would discuss this again after I had more time to gather my thoughts. "All I have are nightgowns. Everything else is too small," I said.

"Okay, then, I'll have to have my mother bring you something because you can't wear a nightgown with guests here. I'm so glad you and Marcus are back together. I hope he can be faithful, but if he can't, have you . . . ever considered an open relationship? People do it all the time, you know. As long as you have his heart, what does it matter if another woman has his body?"

This child was stuck on stupid. "Get me some ice water!" I yelled.

"Huh? Why are you yelling? Are you okay?"

"Yes, but suddenly, I'm just very thirsty, and this room temp water isn't quenching it. Please go to the kitchen and get me a glass of ice water with lots and lots of ice." I started fanning myself profusely with my hands. "Go now."

Mia obliged and promptly left the room. While she was gone I went in her purse and took out my keys. If that was how she was going to use my car, there was no way I could continue to let her keep it. But how was I going to confiscate my keys without telling Marcus or Mrs. Colbert why I did it?

She returned a few minutes later with a large cup of ice water, and I greedily gulped it down. I drank it so fast some of it dribbled down my chin and onto my night-gown. After I drank every last bit, I told her to plug up the curlers so I could curl my hair. I had a feeling this baby shower was going to be more than any of us bargained for. The least I could do was look like I'm ready for anything.

Chapter 20

Marcus

I must admit that it felt good to be back in a good place with Natalie. For the majority of this pregnancy we've been at each other's throat so much, I was beginning to question if I would be able to *actually* be the type of father I wanted to be. I began to think about all the broken homes I either witnessed or heard about growing up. Some of the stories consisted of situations where the mother and father were so turned off by each other that the kid suffered the most. Sadly, that's why most men tend to run from their respective responsibilities. Some men can't sit in a "heated" kitchen with a woman, so they decide to leave that kitchen. I have some friends who have told me all kinds of horror stories of their dreadful experiences with the mothers of their children: from them using the kids as bargaining chips to the women acting like spawns of the devil—just pure evilness. However, I realize that's only *their* side of the story. I know my bros, and *trust* me, they're not innocent beings. I'm sure they contributed to a lot of the craziness they were involved in. Hell, just look at my situation with Natalie. It speaks for itself.

It was nice to step away for a minute to gather my thoughts. After tussling with Jackson, I can say that I was a little relieved. I'd been having so much pent-up frustration and energy as of late, it was alleviating to release some of it. However, I will admit that I felt a little bad about the entire ordeal. I mean, he *was* considered to be someone I called my brother. Even with his flaws and sneak moves, I still had love for him. What can I say? I'm a loyal dude to a fault.

As I was sitting in traffic, I turned up the radio to listen to my favorite personality discuss the upcoming presidential election. I can honestly say that my energy to vote in this election was being drained day by day. Neither party member was speaking or addressing the issues that mattered to me and my people in the community. It was becoming a spectacle, almost similar to a scripted wrestling or comedic show.

I leaned over to get a glimpse of my lip in the rear-view mirror. Jackson punched me pretty good. A burning sensation sent a slight chill through my body as I licked the swollen area for a little lubrication. I know once my mother sees this, she is going to act a fool, especially if I decide to tell her why.

I felt my phone vibrate in my pants pocket. I pulled it out and after looking at the screen, a slight smirk began to form on my face.

"Speak of the devil," I said as I answered.

"Boy, don't you be wishing Satan on me."

I laughed. "What's up, Momma? What can I do for you?"

She began to give me the rundown of *her* checklist of items for me to get. When she planned something, she wanted it done *her* way or no way. I didn't attempt to put up a fight. Now I see why my dad was so passive when I was growing up. Besides, what did I know about baby showers.

After almost five minutes of talking with no breaks in between, she said, "I need you to do me one more favor."

"What's that?"

"I'm still helping Mrs. Baker pick these greens, so I won't be able to—let me stop lying—I don't *want* to go all the way across town to pick your father up. Can you do that on your way back to Natalie's place?"

"Sure thing. I can do that. Tell Mrs. Baker I said hello."

My mother then did what I hated the most. "You can tell her yourself."

Before I got a chance to make any type of rebuttal, Mrs. Baker was on the phone. I grunted underneath my breath a little as I knew this was not just going to be a simple hi-and-bye situation. Mrs. Baker was a sweet woman, but she could gossip her ass off. After about an additional 5 minutes of listening to her jibber jabber, I blew the horn on my car and lied. "Sorry, Mrs. Baker . . . These people are blowing at me. I can't talk and drive. Talk to you later." After I said my good-byes, I hung up the phone quicker than a man sinking in quicksand.

I got off at the next exit en route to pick up my father. It was hard to believe that I was about to be a father myself. I couldn't imagine—*me*—Marcus Colbert—a dad. I was ready and willing, but it was still surreal nevertheless.

As I pulled up into the driveway, I noticed that Natalie had left me a couple of text messages: Be sure to get me some strawberries, saltine crackers, and liver cheese.

I cringed when I read liver cheese. It had been years since I'd had the displeasure of eating some. When I was younger, it was amazing, but as I grew more mature, so did my taste buds.

***

I marveled at the upkeep of my parents' lawn as I knocked on the door. With my head facing the street, I began to look out and reminisce about the good ol' days: playing street ball, basketball, and other boyhood games with my father. I smiled. I was envisioning me and my son playing in that same street and yard one day—creating our own memories.

My father opened the door looking like he was headed to a funeral.

"Dad, why you all jazzed up? It's just a baby shower."

"Well, you never know. I figure if that baby drops, I want him to see how clean his G-Daddy is."

"G-Daddy?" I quizzed with an inquisitive look on my face.

He laughed. "What's wrong with that name?"

Now, laughing myself, I shook my head and replied, "Nothing, Pops, nothing at all."

As we escaped the darkness of the living room, his eyes caught a glimpse of my face.

"What happened to you, boy? Natalie finally decided to knock some sense into you?" Noticing that I was no longer laughing or smiling, he said, "Oh boy . . . This is serious, ain't it? Boy, I hope you ain't went and had a physical altercation with that girl. I swear if you—"

I put up my hands and halted my father from continuing, "Chill, chill, Pops. It's nothing like that."

"Well, what is it?"

I proceeded to explain the entire situation.

"I knew that boy was a black heron," my father said.

With my brows curling up, I replied, "What does that mean?"

"A black heron is an African water bird. It means he's conniving. He's a canopy feeder. He seeks out his prey by providing them with a false sense of security in the form of *friendship,* and then he strikes."

I nodded my head as if I understood his rhetoric.

"Well, I'm glad no one was seriously hurt in this situation."

"Yeah, just a bunch of egos, I suppose," I replied.

My father's strong hands gripped down on my shoulders. "Well, son, let's hit this road before your mother sends another list of commands."

After going to several stores to get everything on my mother's list, we returned to Natalie's house to find my mother had commandeered the kitchen. I noticed that my sister was nestled in the corner of the room with her face deep in her phone and her lip all poked out. My mother yelled at her to get off the phone and help. I could tell something was bothering her, so I decided to show her some brotherly love.

"What's wrong? Having boyfriend issues?" I began to tease.

She rolled her eyes and tried her best to ignore her annoying big brother. When I figured that my presence was not welcomed, I proceeded to walk to the kitchen with the others. Just as I was in full stride, she said, "Nat took back her keys from me!"

I turned. I wasn't too surprised. Natalie had been complaining about her not responding to her calls or text messages in a timely manner. I wondered if it had anything to do with her taking her care to Murfreesboro. "Oh yeah? And why did she do that?"

I wasn't expecting any type of truth or acknowledgment of fault to escape her lips. After all, she was still a teenager, and the majority of them can't seem to find the error of their ways. So she did what most spoiled kids did . . . She hunched her shoulders and said with the ugliest of ugly looks and said, "I'on know!"

Sarcastically, I replied, "Sure, you don't." I continued, "Well, I'm sure me and Natalie will talk about it later. I'll see what I can do about getting you back the keys. Before I do that, is there something you need to prepare me for or tell me first?"

No reply from her, just a loud exhale of annoyance escaped her teenage body.

I was then summoned by my mother to get in the kitchen to help with the food as if that was my specialty. My mother was the type of person who just wanted people to look busy, even if they didn't know what the hell they were doing. So, I did as I was told and proceeded to *look* the part in the kitchen. After years of experience, my dad already stood in formation. He was sitting quiet as a mouse cracking eggs in a bowl. My mother suddenly looked in my father's direction and said, "Montgomery, why the hell you cracking all them eggs?" He looked up, looked at me, then proceeded to look at my mother and just shrugged his shoulders. They were hilarious at times.

***

Less than 2 hours later, the apartment was full of jolly family and friends. Torn envelops with cards sticking out of some and not others were all over the floor. Shreds of wrapping paper were overflowing the kitchen garbage can accompanied by food residue-stained paper plates. Laughter and clapping hands had become the soundtrack for the evening. Smiles and tears were the rhythm for some, as joy and sadness were the blues for others. The evening was a showcase of all emotions imaginable.

The tunes of my mother and father's era were blasting from the speaker. The old lady from upstairs kept banging down on the ceiling to quiet us down. The commotion would calm down for a minute, and then just like an old engine, it would rev right back up.

My phone buzzed again. It was Chanel. She had been calling me for the past hour back to back. I texted her and told her I was busy and couldn't talk, but that didn't keep her from texting. Now that Natalie and I were back on good terms, I was not about to get put in the doghouse for being inattentive. Right now, she was the only woman that mattered.

I glanced at my phone and saw the following message:

I REALLY NEED TO TALK TO YOU.

I initially wasn't going to respond, but Chanel and I left our last conversation on such good terms that I owed her a line of communication. After all, she too was expecting a child with me. I responded:

I WILL GIVE YOU A CALL AS SOON AS I CAN. IS EVERYTHING OKAY?

Chanel: MARCUS, YOU KNOW I WOULDN'T BE SO DETERMINED TO REACH YOU IF IT WASN'T IMPORTANT. PLEASE CALL ME ASAP!!!

Marcus: OKAY. I WILL. I'M AT NATALIE'S PLACE RIGHT NOW. I DON'T WANT TO CAUSE A SCENE, SO AS SOON AS I CAN STEP AWAY, I'LL CALL.

Chanel: YOU KNOW WHAT . . . DON'T WORRY ABOUT IT. I NOW KNOW WHERE YOUR PRIORITIES STAND.

Marcus: I'M JUST TRYING TO HANDLE THE SITUATION THE BEST WAY I KNOW HOW. WE DISCUSSED THIS ALREADY. I THOUGHT WE WERE ON THE SAME PAGE. WAS I MISTAKEN?

So much for honesty. She didn't respond back. It must not have been much of an emergency. *I'll have to deal with whatever it is later*, I thought to myself. I wasn't completely honest with Natalie earlier when I told her what Chanel and I talked about. We actually discussed giving it another try as she didn't want to be an unwed mother. However, so much damage had been done on both sides that we, or more accurately I, decided that wouldn't be wise. I damaged that relationship, and I was man enough to say no, because I knew it potentially wouldn't end well. She and I never should have happened. She was Lisa's friend, and I already had a baby on the way with another woman. I had to start doing things the right way. Initially, she didn't take it too well, but we talked some more, and I thought we left on good terms.

Chanel is a strong woman. She's beautiful with a great head on her shoulders. She was excelling in the corporate world and in the community. She was almost like a chocolate-covered Lisa with a few more curves. It didn't help that her father is the pastor of one of the most prominent churches in the city. It doesn't look good that not only is the dutiful daughter pregnant, but her child's father is nowhere in the picture. I've never been much for keeping up appearances, and I definitely wasn't going to start now.

I turned my attention back to the baby shower. I looked at my mother sitting angelic, just having a good ol' time. I began to think about the times we shared in my youthful years. I was proud and privileged to have a mother like her. I then stared down my father. He was the captain of the ship. He had his arm draped around my mother, and it seemed as if he was whispering sweet nothings into her ear. I loved the fact that they *still* loved each other. Finally, my eyes found Natalie. She had been the tearful one the entire night. My heart was melting for her. I was feeling it, and it was feeling—real. She caught me looking. A smile formed on her face. She blew me a kiss, and I caught it as if it was our little secret. She looked beautiful. Her hair had grown quite a bit during the pregnancy and after my sister flat-ironed it, it hung past her shoulders. She was wearing some type of wreathe on her head with *mommy-to-be* on it. I found it in a store and lied and told her I made it as a joke. She actually believed me! Ha! I'll tell the truth later. She seemed to enjoy seeing some of her church members and a couple of girls from the office where she used to work. Her brother's girlfriend was there too, but Jessie and Manny opted not to come. I don't think they're ready to face me now that I know they were the ones who jumped me. My father and I were actually the only men there.

Some time had passed before I heard a subtle knock at the door. Leaving the laughter and love, I headed toward the door. I looked back for another glimpse of the love that was within that apartment before I proceeded to open it. As I pulled the door open, my eyes widened. The next thing I saw was a flash of light that was red like fire. My ears were ringing. My body was warm all over. I began to have heat flashes. I was having trouble breathing. As I was losing consciousness, the laughter and joy began to fade in that small apartment. It was now replaced by the sound of moving chairs, broken glasses, broken voices, and screams of terror. Then, my world and the world around me went black.

Chapter 21

Natalie

This can't be happening. One moment I'm laughing and sipping on a virgin margarita and the next I'm staring at the father of my child on the floor and he's not moving. Someone yelled, "He's been shot!" I screamed. His parents rushed to his side.

"Baby, get up!" I yelled. I saw blood begin to cover his chest. I tried to move and go to him but no sooner than my enlarged behind left the oversized armchair I was sitting in, my water broke. It was followed by a sharp pain shooting through my abdomen. I screamed and rubbed my stomach. This was too much! The baby can't come now. I needed Marcus by my side in the delivery room. I began hyperventilating. Mrs. Colbert left her son and rushed to my side.

"Breathe, child," she instructed.

"Marcus, get up!" I screamed. "Our child is coming. I need you. You're going to miss the birth of our son."

I heard him moan.

Mia was on the phone with 911 frantically trying to tell them what was needed. Her voice was two octaves higher than usual. "We need an ambulance now! My brother has been shot!" Mrs. Colbert yelled out, "We need two. Natalie is in labor!"

I looked at her like I didn't want to believe the words coming out of her mouth. She kept talking. "Natalie! Marcus is in no condition to help you right now. Get it together. Your child needs you. With or without my son you *can* deliver this baby."

Without Marcus. The concept seemed foreign to me. We may have had our problems, but after my initial false labor I never once imagined ushering Trenton into the world without his daddy. Except when I got mad at him and wouldn't let him in the delivery room. My body grew heated. I could feel sweat forming on my neck, back, and temples. I snatched off the ring of flowers that was placed on my head earlier. It was a beautiful crown fashioned by the man who said he wanted us to raise our child together as a family. I was princess for a day, and my unborn son was the star, but I guess he didn't feel right not being a physical part of the festivities. Another pain shot through my body.

I could hear Mia in the background yelling my address into the phone. "Who do you want to speak to first? The person attending to the gunshot victim or the woman in labor?"

I looked at Marcus again lying on the floor. He was still motionless. He's got to be all right. I can't raise the baby without him. I grabbed an empty paper plate near me and began fanning myself. My wet dress clung to me around my thighs and buttocks.

"Get me some water," I heard Mrs. Colbert yell.

I tried to say thank you. I heard myself say "th—," and then the room went black.

***

I woke up in the hospital. I was lying down with my head on a pillow. I blinked rapidly as I looked straight up in the air at the white ceiling and bright lights. They were way too bright and hurt my eyes. I closed them momentarily before shifting my gaze in the direction of the soft noises I heard from the monitors to my right. I tried to focus and noticed the lines that represented two heartbeats. One was mine, and one was my baby's. I felt a sharp pain shoot through me again and one of the lines climbed upward.

I heard someone to my left move. "There you are," said Mrs. Colbert. "I didn't know it was possible for someone to go into labor while they were unconscious, but, child, you did just that. You fainted and had us all worried you wouldn't wake up in time to give birth." She chuckled. "You have dilated four centimeters. It seems Trenton is finally ready to make his arrival."

I rubbed my swollen belly, and then called on Jesus as another contraction jolted through me. "Where's Marcus?" I screeched.

"He's here in the hospital." Even in my drug-induced state I could tell she was hiding something. I looked at her. Her eyes were red and swollen, like she had been crying quite a bit.

"What's wrong?"

She took a deep breath. "Don't worry about me. It's been an emotional day. My son gets shot. My future daughter-in-law goes into labor. An old woman can only take so much, but I'll be fine. I'm a tough old broad." She tried to force a laugh, but it came out more like a grunt.

"I'm not having this baby without him," I said matter-of-factly.

"Natalie, I don't think you have a choice. He's in no condition to be by your side right now. He's been shot. You were there. We have no idea who did it. Why would anyone want to hurt my child?" She patted my hand and sniffed. We heard the door to the room open, and we both turned our heads to see someone in the doorway. He was tall and dressed in all black. "Marcus?" I said. My eyes were still adjusting to the light so it took me a minute to focus.

"Perhaps I could be of some assistance?" he said.

I recognized the voice immediately. "What are you doing here?" I asked.

"I came to your house to apologize to you and Marcus and the few people who were there cleaning up told me what happened. I rushed down here to check on both of you. I know I'm not Marcus, but I'm here if you need me."

"It is very nice of you to apologize, but I won't be needing you. My Marcus will be here. Only death could keep him from seeing his first child being born."

Mrs. Colbert and Jackson looked at each other. She opened her mouth to say something, then closed it. She licked her lips and started over. I could tell she was choosing her words carefully. "Natalie, Marcus is not well. He's lost a lot of blood. He's in critical condition and unable to come."

I smiled. "He'll be here. I've got six more centimeters to go before I have this baby. He'll be here. Jackson, you can leave. I don't want you here when Marcus arrives. Better yet, I have an idea. Since he can't come to me, I'll go to him. Help me get out of this bed into a chair and take me to his room."

Mrs. Colbert looked at me like I had lost my mind and said, "I wouldn't advise it. My son isn't doing well."

I rolled my eyes. "Oh, you thought I was making a request?" I said. I reached for the call button and pushed it. A friendly nurse with a high squeaky voice answered, "Hello. How can I help you?"

"I need to speak to my attending physician immediately."

"Is there something wrong, ma'am?"

"Hell, yeah! Now get me my damn doctor!" I screamed.

Chapter 22

Marcus

I've always been told that before you die, you'll see your life flash before your eyes. I wasn't expecting to be testing that theory anytime soon, but with life you have to always expect the unexpected.

I couldn't comprehend what was going on. I was feeling empty and light on the inside as if the law of gravity had failed me. I was awake consciously, but physically, I was unable to move. I was crying on the inside. I was praying for forgiveness for all the wrong I'd done to myself and others. My body felt cold and stiff. My memory would constantly drift. I was fighting to keep control of my mind. I was fighting to control my body. Ultimately, I was fighting to live.

My world continued to be black. I could hear voices from a distance. The muffled sounds began to startle me as I was trying hard to recognize the voice and words. The harder I tried, the faster my heart began to beat. At that moment, I could hear subtle beeping noises that began to beep at a rapid pace. Those muffled voices drew closer. I could feel a presence surrounding me. *This is what faith feels like*, I said to myself. To actually *feel* something and know it's real without *seeing* it.

More commotion began to scatter throughout my mind: more voices—more unfamiliar sounds. Frustration was building within me. I wanted to say something. I wanted to know. I wanted to live.

My memory had forsaken me, but for a moment, the voices and words became clear as day: *"You can't be in here. Please go back to your room. I'm begging you. Somebody call Dr. Ellis . . ."*

Then I heard, *"Marcus, please wake up . . . please!!!"*

I began to fight more as I recognized that voice and the pain within it.

"Ma'am, you can't be in here. You're exciting the patient which is not a good thing. And you can cause stress and harm to yourself and your child."

"I have to be in here. I can't leave. I won't leave," Natalie replied with desperation and pleading in her voice.

In a split second I couldn't hear her anymore. *Has my memory forsaken me again?* I thought to myself. I began trying to fight some more. My heart rate accelerated. New voices entered the room. There were more loud beeps from the machine. I could now hear screams. Someone was endangered or hurt. I began to fight.

"Calm down, Mr. Colbert. We're losing him!" My chest was expanded as impulses and shock waves were maneuvering through my body. "Come on, Mr. Colbert—fight. We need more hands on deck, PLEASE." I was fighting, but I was beginning to lose the battle. "We have to open him up now. We can't wait any longer. Somebody please get this young lady out of here. We can't do our job with her here."

So, I guess this is it. My cycle of life was coming to an end. Just when I thought I had it all together, it was snatched from me like a thief in the night. The hardest part about saying good-bye is not having the opportunity to do so. I prepared myself and became at peace with it all. But then it hit me. I'd never get to hold my son, play ball with him in my parents' yard, or show Trenton how to be a good man. I'd never get to propose to Natalie and watch her eyes sparkle as beautiful as the rock I would have placed on her finger. We wouldn't have our first dance at our wedding or stand with tears in our eyes as our child graduated from college. As my memory began to fade again, so did my soul. I was sorry for the things I'd done and I desperately wanted to make it right. I began to feel light again . . . free . . . empty. My black world became blacker—then silence . . .

Book III Sneak Peek

Chapter One

Natalie

"PUSH!! And BREATHE! We're almost there!" said the doctor. My OBGYN couldn't get here in time so there's some man I never met, all in my twat guiding me and my little one. He sounded like a drill sergeant as he forcefully instructed me how to bring life into the world at a time when all I wanted to do was die.

I'm in no shape to be delivering a baby. The love of my life is in another part of the hospital fighting for his life, and here I am bringing life forth without him. I didn't mean to upset Marcus. I just wanted to see my man, my baby daddy, the man I wanted to spend the rest of my life with. It didn't help that as they rolled me out, I saw Chanel standing outside the door. I wanted to roll that wheelchair right over her foot and kick her in the shin. I knew the only person that could have told her was Jackson. That man is so conniving. He had the nerve to try to be in the delivery room with me. No way!

I was silently praying while I was pushing. *Father God, please let Marcus be okay. Neither one of us has been perfect, but we are just starting to get it right. Have mercy on him.*

"You're doing just fine, Natalie . . . NOW PUSH!!" the doctor instructed.

I bore down as hard as I could and gave a thrust to the lower half of my abdomen. I couldn't really feel the lower half of my body thanks to the epidural but sweat was continuously rolling off the upper half.

"Now, one more big one should do it!"

I did as I was instructed. A few seconds later he said, "Here—" then the doctor cut his sentence short.

I didn't hear any crying. There should be crying . . . shouldn't there? I looked up at Mrs. Colbert. She hadn't said much. I knew she was mad at me for upsetting Marcus, but at least she was there. Even in her anger she hadn't abandoned me in my time of need. She gave me a forced smile as she wiped the sweat from my brow with a damp cloth. I opened my mouth to ask what was wrong, but I suddenly felt a tightness in my chest, like someone had their fist wrapped around my heart. She suddenly looked in the direction of the doctor and stopped. Her stoic smile disappeared, and her face now held great concern.

"Code Blue. She's going into cardiac arrest!" I heard the doc say.

"Stay with me, Natalie," said Mrs. Colbert. She said something else after that, but it was low and garbled. She was standing right next to me, but she sounded far away.

Suddenly, I saw a blinding bright light. Then, in the glow appeared the glorious figure of a man. I couldn't quite recognize him, but the silhouette appeared to be that of . . . Marcus? It can't be.

Did I just die? Lord, help!

About the Authors

Jae Henderson

Jae Henderson's writing exists to motivate others. She invites readers to join her on a most entertaining journey that imparts some sage wisdom and assists readers in further realizing that we may not be perfect, but we serve a perfect God. Now the author of five books, she began in 2011 with her debut inspirational romance novel, *Someday*. In 2012, she released the sequel, *Someday, Too,* and followed it with the finale to her trilogy, *Forever and a Day* in 2013. She followed those with two books of inspirational short stories, *Things Every Good Woman Should Know, Volume 1 and 2.*

Jae is a graduate of the University of Memphis where she earned a BA in communications and an MA in English. She is the former host and producer of *On Point*, a once popular talk show geared toward youth and young adults. Other accomplishments have included serving as a contributing writer for the award-winning, syndicated *Tom Joyner Morning Show* and a successful career as a voice-over artist. Her signature voice has been heard in hundreds of commercials and even a couple of cartoons. When Jae isn't writing, she works as a public relations specialist. She currently resides in her hometown of Memphis, Tennessee.

Mario D. King

Mario D. King writes to change the world with works that will spark an educational revolution. He made his literary debut in 2013 with the release of his hip-hop novella, *The Crisis Before Midlife*. Met with rave reviews by readers, he decided to continue to encourage change in the community through literature with the release of his first nonfiction project, *What's Happening Brother: How to strategize in a system designed for you to fail.* In it, Mario provides a realistic discourse that embraces accountability and responsibility to systematically address the problems ailing the black community. Through his meticulous research, he explores solutions in education, entrepreneurship, leadership, community, and spirituality, amongst several other topics, to transform the thinking of black men and their respective counterparts. His love for the black family propelled him to embark on a different kind of journey with *Where Do We Go from Here?* King hopes that by helping to illustrate how misguided relationships can negatively affect the lives of all involved, people will make wiser decisions and strengthen black families.

Mario received his bachelor's degree in communications from the University of Tennessee at Chattanooga where he studied global culture and communication, psychology and sociology. He received his MBA from Kaplan University and will continue to stir up change and motivate those with whom he comes in contact. A native of Memphis, Tennessee, this husband and father of three now lives in Charlotte, North Carolina, where he continues to be a positive influence in his community.

Made in the
USA
Lexington, KY